WHEN HOPE WENT SOUTH

A Dart River Novel

PATRICIA SNELLING

AF249336

Published in New Zealand by Inthelight Publishers

Copyright Patricia Snelling 2018

All rights reserved. No portion of this book may be reproduced, stored in a retrieval system, or transmitted in any form or by any means; electronic, mechanical, photocopy, recording, scanning, or other-except for brief quotations in critical reviews or articles, without the prior written permission of the publisher.

This is a work of fiction. Any resemblance to actual persons, living or dead, or actual events is purely coincidental and not to be construed as real.

Scripture quotations are taken from the Holy Bible, New International Version® NIV® Copyright © 1973, 1978, 1984 by International Bible Society. Used by permission of Zondervan. All rights reserved worldwide.

National Library of New Zealand 2018
ISBN: 978-0-473-46355-7
Paperback

Harold Joyce Cover Art
Martin Joyce Graphic Design

Thank you to all the members of my online groups who have assisted me with editing, proofreading, and constructive critique. I am grateful for your encouragement and support.
A special thanks to Judith Little from Auckland who has helped me so much with my writing. Thank you Judith for believing in me, for your dedication and the time you spent in helping me succeed in fulfilling my aspirations as a writer.

Other Books by Author:

Broken Web
Rescue Net
Missing On Kawau

FOLLOW ME:
https://www.facebook.com/PatriciaSnellingAuthor
https://www.patriciasnelling.com/

Chapter One

A Little Town Called Bethlehem
Bay of Plenty, New Zealand 1971

Frank Petersen tottered down the path towards the front door of Number 10 Penny Lane. He coughed and spluttered, stopped to get his breath then sloped forward, tripping as he climbed the steps. He almost toppled backwards as his legs threatened to buckle. He blindly fumbled in his pocket for his key with one hand while grabbing the handrail with the other before he inserted the metal into the lock. The key failed to find its destination as the door swung open.

Myra, his wife, appeared holding the door wide open. He lurched forward, almost landing on the dining table.

'There you are. Paralytic again. Your food's in the oven and probably dried up by now. I don't know why I even bother cooking for you.'

Hope listened to the shuffling and bumping. He was drunk again she was sure. The squeak of the front door made her hold her breath.

More shuffling and a crash. She wondered what he'd stumbled into this time. Tomorrow he'll probably forget how he got the bruises.

Hope pulled the blankets over her head, her stomach tensing. She didn't want to hear the yelling and ugly words. Inky slid under the duvet and rubbed her nose on Hope's cheek. The softness of the black cat offered a bit of comfort, but it didn't stop the angry words bouncing off the walls of the small house. When will this end? She can't stand much more of this. Her faithful companion's fur soaked up her tears until sleep pulled her into oblivion.

Doug would be home today. Although he was ten years older than Hope, he never treated her like a bothersome little sister. He was her friend and protector. Even after serving in Vietnam as a radiographer and returning home changed. Broken. That's the word she'd use. He even drank like her dad. Never as much, though.

Sitting by the window made her feel closer to him as she imagined him on his way home for a short leave from the hospital in Auckland. Was he still on the plane? Or had he left the airport already, making the last short trek to their house?

'Hope! Come here and help me with this chicken. You can sew it up with this when you've finished stuffing it.' Her mother handed her a needle and thread and a bowl of herbs with breadcrumbs. 'You'll need an egg to bind it, remember?'

'What time is Doug arriving? I can't wait to see him.' She parted the Venetian blinds and looked down the driveway.

'He'll be here soon— that's if the shuttle from the airport doesn't do a big round trip. After you've finished stuffing the chicken you could set the table for dinner.'

'I hear a car. I think it's the shuttle.' Hope rushed to the sink and rinsed her hands under the tap. She wiped them on her jeans and dashed to the door. 'Come on Mum. Let's go to the gate and meet him.'

Her mother scooted to the mirror in the hallway. She pushed at her auburn curls that wouldn't behave then hurried to the back door and yelled out.

'Frank, come inside. Doug's here.'

Too late. Doug had turned the corner of the house with Hope hanging onto his sleeve. Taking two steps at a time she rushed up the front stairs, her arm looped through Doug's almost pulling him off balance. Her face brimmed with a smile like a toothpaste advert. Doug stopped as his father grunted something from behind and plodded towards him. Doug turned to greet him.

'Dad. How are you?' His father put out his hand. Instead of shaking it, as usual, Doug ignored it and put his hand inside his jacket. He extracted a packet of Tasman Light pipe tobacco.

'Gee, thanks, boy. I've just run out of the stuff.' He took a deep whiff. 'Smells good.' As Frank continued to sniff the tobacco loudly, his wife pushed past him to get at Doug. She threw her arms around him then stood back, looking him up and down.

'What have they been feeding you? Wasting away to a shadow again, I see. I'll have to fix that.'

Hope knew by the way Myra had always doted on Doug, that he was the apple of her eye. She dragged Doug by the hand through into the lounge. He stripped off his brown corduroy jacket and slumped into the leather couch. Hope plonked herself down next to him, about to fire questions at him about his leave. Myra entered the lounge and glared disapprovingly at Hope.

'Help me bring in the tea trolley, please. Pop the scones underneath. There's a pot of raspberry jam on the bench.'

Hope trundled back in with the trolley to see her mother had hogged Doug's attention. As usual, Frank shrunk into a seat in the corner of the room while Myra handed everyone a plate.

'Help yourselves. I'm done for the day.' She dumped herself in her special armchair and leaned forward rubbing the side of her foot. 'Must get these awful shoes off soon.'

'This is very formal. I don't usually get scones on arrival.' Doug had guzzled a whole scone. He pulled out his handkerchief and wiped jam from the corner of his mouth. Hope handed him a paper serviette.

'It was Hope's idea because you haven't been home in ages. She had me making scones early this morning.' Myra gave a half smile.

'How long are you home this time?' Frank finally got a word in.

'Not long. I go back in a week. I'm on call after this and we're flat out. Lots of staff off sick.'

***

Doug's leave had flown by and the week was almost out. Not enough time to spend doing the things Hope had planned to do with him. She'd asked him to take her fishing at the beach. There was also the waterhole she had discovered a few weeks ago near Misty's paddock and she'd hoped he would swim there with her. But today was one of the many days when her mother took up his time.

'Sorry, Hope. I promised Mum I'd mow the lawns today. Maybe we could go tomorrow. Dad doesn't do much to help her these days.'

Her head started pounding. She could feel the stress on her amalgam fillings as she clenched her teeth. That's how she'd fractured one of them recently.

'I know that! Dad doesn't help her around here much at all. I'm always finding her up on the roof painting the corrugated iron or mowing lawns and weeding gardens. That's when she's not in the orchard picking fruit or packing tomatoes. She gets so grumpy when she's tired and takes it out on me. Dad just disappears somewhere between the tomato rows until dusk to stay out of her way.'

Doug put his arm around her shoulders, leaning gently on her. 'I know sweetie. That's why I need to help her when I'm at home.'

The resentment burnt a hole in her soul. If it wasn't for her Dad's drinking, she could have had a fun holiday with Doug. It had always been the same whether her father was drunk or sober. This was her lot. Will it ever change? Perhaps it's time to escape it all.

***

Thank goodness for the Returned Servicemen's reunion. Hope and Doug had barely had five minutes alone together since he'd arrived home. Now they had a whole evening ahead of them. She raced down the hall from her room and stopped short. She'd planned a night of card games with her big brother, but his furrowed brow and tight lips didn't look like anticipation. They spelt angst.

'There's something I think I need to tell you, something important.' He patted the seat next to him on the couch.

'What do you mean? What's up?'

'I'm telling you this because you'll soon be leaving school and you've already told me you want to go places, find work, and go to university.'

'What are you trying to say, Doug?'

'Something Dad said to me in one of his drunken states one night. You know how verbal he gets when he's been drinking.' His voice croaked as if he was struggling to get the words out. He locked her gaze. 'He told me that you're not his daughter and that it's always been a family secret.'

Hope leapt to her feet. Her stomach heaved as she swallowed the remains of her last meal that lingered in her stomach, burning her throat. 'What are you talking about? He was just drunk and probably talking rubbish.'

He reached out to her, taking her hand.

'It's true. He confirmed it one day when he was sober and told me I must never tell you or anyone else. He said he should never have told me.'

She fought back tears. 'I knew there was something wrong. All my life I believed I was adopted or perhaps a foster child. I knew I didn't fit in.' She clenched her fists. 'Why didn't Mum tell me all these years? I wouldn't have had to find out like this.' She wiped her glass-like tears with her sleeve as they scalded her hot cheeks.

'Do you know who my real father is? Please, Doug! I have to know. Please tell me!' She pulled on his arm, glaring at him bug-eyed.

'I can only guess who it is, but I have no evidence. I might be wrong, then I'll be in trouble. Only Mum can tell you.'

'Well, she won't! She hasn't done all these years, and I'm nearly nineteen years old. I'm going to give her one chance and if she refuses to tell me the truth, I'll leave home!'

Tears welled up in her eyes again. She quickly wiped them and as she looked up at Doug, she could see that his eyes were moist too.

He lowered his head, looking at his feet. Then he stood and wrapped her in a hug. His embrace warmed her but did not fill the new broken places in her heart. She took a step away.

Doug lifted her chin. 'You'd better get to bed now. They'll be back from the reunion soon and it's late. We can talk about it tomorrow.'

Hope sloped off to her bedroom and crashed onto her bed. Her entire body ached, calling out for sleep. Yet it didn't come. She had almost pried the truth out of him, but he was loyal to the end.

Hope's sick of all the arguments when Frank comes home drunk every night. And her mother with all her deceit. How could they keep such a secret all these years? She must get away from it all. She'll have to pick her moment to confront her mother so she won't get Doug into trouble.

Her head almost burst with the pent-up emotion. She struggled to get off to sleep with a throbbing headache, tossing and turning and hoping to be asleep before they arrive home to start the arguments all over again.

***

Finally, school was done. Hope sloped into the living room. Her stomach twisted as she approached her mother.

'Mum—now that school has finished, I'm going to take a gap year. I'll find a job in some stables or do farm work for a year before I go to university.'

Her mother stood in the doorway frowning at her. 'I don't know why you don't want to go nursing. You don't know what's good for you!'

'No, Mum! I told you I'm not interested. Just because you think it's a noble profession, it doesn't mean that I have to take it up!' She stifled the urge to scream at her. 'You can't keep trying to live your broken dreams through me.' Hope crossed her arms in defiance.

Myra scooped up a pile of clothes from the laundry basket, dumping them next to the ironing board.

'It will always provide you with job security and you'll be able to travel all over the world as a nurse.' She slammed the iron down roughly. Hissing steam spat from it like an enraged creature.

'I've made up my mind already. You know my passion is to work with animals. I want to have a career with horses.'

'You'll never get a proper job doing that. I doubt it. In fact, I've already told you that without qualifications you'll become nothing!'

'That's right. That's why I'm doing a diploma that specialises in horse health.'

'What a load of rubbish. You won't get into a university doing something like that.'

'I already have done. I've been accepted for the Diploma in Agriscience Equine in Dunedin. I'm doing it through correspondence. That way, I can do casual work learning to train horses as well.'

'Is that right?' A sneer appeared on Myra's lips. 'You never said anything about it,' she snapped.

Hope rolled her eyes. 'I knew you would try to stop me. I applied for a place when I passed my college exams just to see how far I would get. Look, Mum. You should be happy for me.'

'I didn't see any letters from the university.' Her mother stood stiff, bracing herself with her hands on her hips.

'That's because I had them sent to Jessie's house.' Hope looked down at the floor.

'That was very deceitful, don't you think?'

Hope jerked her head back up and glared at her, anger rekindled.

'No, not deceitful. Cautious. I didn't want you ruining my chances. That would be selfish, don't you think?'

Myra started to back off. She pressed her lips together, as she always did when she was working an impossible problem.

'Well, I've never heard such utter rubbish in all my life. You'll never amount to anything doing that— you mark my words.'

'It would be nice for you to encourage me, just for once. You always put me down.' Hope's eyes blurred.

'Well, I just thought it would be wiser for you to stay and go nursing. You could live at home and save money. Here—take these blouses to your room and hang them up.'

She just wants to keep me here as her slave.

Memories of having a copper for boiling water pushed forward in her mind. Hope hated going into the outside laundry in the old corrugated iron shed where it stood amongst the cobwebs and bugs. She'd felt sorry for Doug, that it was his job to stoke it and carry the scalding hot water into the house for their baths. He'd only been a teenager then but was required to carry the water in the heavy metal buckets three times a week when he arrived home from school. *Well—I'm not going to end up like that. Poor Doug.*

Hope hung up her blouses in her wardrobe and walked back into the dining room. She plopped down at the table, grabbed a rag and started cleaning the heavy Venetian blinds each blade one by one. This was her mother's favourite job for her. She drew her brows together and narrowed her eyes. She was a slave. She worked and worked and received no reward. Her pockets were still bare at the end of it.

She threw the cloth down. 'I know that Frank isn't my real father. And I need to know the truth.'

'What? Where did you get that? Who's been talking to you?'

'Frank in one of his drunken stupors spilt the beans. Why did I have to find out this way? You've both deceived me.' Hope's tone was brusque. She swallowed around the lump in her throat and blinked back tears, willing herself not to break down. It was no good. She cracked. Tears gushed down her face. She grabbed a tissue from her pocket, blew her nose, and shoved her fringe roughly out of her eyes.

Her mother blew on her glasses that appeared fogged and wiped them with the corner of her blouse. Her lips pursed. She glowered at Hope then shifted her gaze straight ahead. Frozen tears filled her eyes.

'He's talking rubbish. Anything comes out of him when he's drunk.'

'I believe him. Why would he say that if I was his daughter? You're lying. If you don't tell me the truth, I'm leaving home … for good.' Hope stood up abruptly, pushing her chair back.

'Anyway – I've decided to go away for a month or so. Jessie's father has some farm work for me until I get a regular job. I have some thinking to do.'

'When are you going? This is ridiculous.' Her mother barked.

'Jessie's picking me up in the morning. If you don't tell me the truth before I leave, I'll be thinking about moving out when I get back.'

'Moving … where? You're overreacting!'

'Overreacting— you're in denial. How can you say such a thing?'

'I don't know what you're talking about.' Myra persisted. 'You're overreacting to something you don't understand. Oh well—if that's the way you want to go.'

'I want to save some money before I commence my studies in a year. I'll be looking for a proper job while I'm staying with them.'

Hope stormed off into her room. *Over-reacting she says. Now I know I have to get out of here.*

Hope lay on her bed thinking how different family life was at Jessie's house. Mental weariness drained today's events out of her. Sleep was an attractive proposition and oblivion came quickly.

Awakening feeling unrefreshed the next morning, she could smell the aroma of fresh toast emanating from the kitchen. She bolted her breakfast down, then dressed, and went outside looking for Frank. She thought it best to tell him she was off to Jessie's for a month.

Myra hung her head out the kitchen window.

'Hope— I need to talk to you before you go,' she bellowed.

Frank kept his head down as he continued to hoe the trenches he'd prepared for planting the potatoes. It was as if he knew there was trouble brewing but said little to her. 'Off you go then. Try not to upset your mother and let her know your plans.'

As if he really cared about her plans. Hope cleverly hid her lack of respect for him for not having the spine to bring the truth out into the open. But deep down, she felt sorry for him.

She went back inside to fetch her backpack and dumped it at the front door. 'What is it, Mum? Jessie will be here soon.' She thought her mother was about to confess. Or was it just wishful thinking.

'What are you going to do about Misty while you're away?' Hope's neck tensed. Her mother was still in denial.

'Someone needs to keep an eye on her and check her water trough. I can't. I'm busy with the Women's Institute fundraising this month.' Myra's nose twitched, the way it always did when she justified her behaviour.

'Peter said he'll look out for her. You know— Joel's friend in the carpentry workshop whom he used to work with. He loves horses and knows Misty well.'

'But he isn't there all the time. He only works part-time like Joel used to.'

'That's okay. Misty has everything she needs. She just has to be checked every few days.'

'I'm glad that's all sorted then. It's been years since I've had to handle a horse.' Myra scowled at her.

A horn tooted outside on the street. Jessie was there. Hope gave her mother a quick peck on the cheek and met her gaze. 'Please, Mum, do the right thing.' As Hope turned to walk out the door, she saw that Myra's eyes had lost all expression.

***

Jessie's parents, Wyatt and Prue Lee owned a large cattle farm on the outskirts of Bethlehem and welcomed Hope with open

12

arms. Hope counted on Wyatt giving her work and references. She was sure she could convince him she was a top-notch farm worker. Thank God he was giving her the chance. She arose each morning when the rooster crowed and worked from daylight to dusk to prove to him her worth.

One evening, when Jessie's parents were in bed, Hope opened up to Jessie. She poured her heart out to her about the devastating revelation that Frank was not her biological father and how Doug blew the whistle on his parent's deception.

'It was pretty selfish your mother not telling you who your real father is all these years. Especially after you begged her.' Jessie put an arm across Hope's shoulders.

'She's scared of a scandal, Doug says. It has been the family secret for years.' Hope started wringing her hands.

'They talked until late into the night stuffing themselves with Fanta, popcorn, and chocolate.

'Jessie—there's something else … something that I'm worried about. But I suppose you want to go off to sleep now.' Jessie had returned to Hope's room in her winceyette pyjamas covered in Panda bears.

'No, I'm fine, really I am. Wait— I'll make us some hot chocolate. I'll bring it in here.'

Hope got ready for bed. She pulled out a photo of Misty from her backpack. Her eyes became glazed, like deep blue glass marbles. They filled with tears and she quickly put the photo back as Jessie walked in with the hot drinks.

'Are you okay, Hope?'

'Oh— I'm fine. Just a bit of hay fever I get at this time of the year.'

'What did you want to tell me?' She placed a mug of steaming hot chocolate milk on the bedside table next to Hope and plonked herself down on the bed next to her.

'It's Doug. There's something wrong with him.'

'What do you mean ... is he sick?'

'Kind of. He was in the permanent army from the age of seventeen and you already know he's a Vietnam War veteran. When he left the army, he was psychologically damaged. His personality has completely changed.'

'Poor Doug. Can't he get some help?'

'He's had a lot of counselling but no one can stop him from getting bad flashbacks. The few times he has come home for a weekend or on holiday, we've been woken by his nightmares. He yells out in his sleep. My room's next to his and it freaks me out.' Hope leaned forward, bracing her arms on her thighs and gazed at the floor. She continued—'One night I saw a flashlight in the hallway and heard him yelling. I got up to find him running around in the dark with a torch and Mum got up to see what the commotion was. He kept on saying, "They're out there ... shush ... they're out there!" He meant that the Viet Cong were outside.'

'Wow! Said Jessie. 'He sounds so messed up. It's so sad. He needs help.'

'He uses alcohol to numb the pain and I think he doesn't care about anything anymore.'

'Would you like me to say a prayer for him? That's all we can really do. I can ask God for a healing of memories. That's what Dad always prays.'

'Thanks Jessie, I'd love that.'

They both closed their eyes while Jessie held her friend's hand and prayed. Afterwards, Jessie wandered back to her own bedroom and as Hope lay in her bed, she had an unusual sense of peace that she had never experienced before.

***

The monthly Farmer's Market was something Hope had not experienced, though she had always wanted to.

She linked arms with Jessie. 'I can't believe I go back home tomorrow. The time's gone by so fast.'

'Nor can I. It's been such fun having you here the last month. I'll miss you. So will Dad. He said you were worth every word he wrote on your reference.'

'I'll miss you, too.' Hope examined the wares of the farmer's market stalls as they strolled, especially the oversized cheeses. She stopped. 'Wait a minute, Jessie. I think she's a girl I know from Pony Club.' She pointed at someone at a stall opposite.

The girl in Jodhpur pants and elaborate looking riding boots walked towards them. She looked up. 'Hope— what are you doing here? I wondered where you had gone. Where's Misty? I rode past her paddock yesterday and couldn't see her. Are you grazing her somewhere else these days?'

'Sally...what? What do you mean? She must be there. I haven't moved her.'

'I had a look around her paddock. Your horse float isn't there either. I thought you must have taken her to a show or a hunt.'

Hope's heart raced. Misty had to be there. She just had to be. 'I'll go back and look for her and make sure. Thanks for that. I've been staying with my friend Jessie for a month and due to return home tomorrow. But I'll have to get back and check on Misty now.'

The two friends said their goodbyes and Jessie led Hope to the market exit. What if Sally was right? She couldn't have escaped

15

by herself. Someone must have let her out. Or taken her. No, it couldn't be. Sally probably just didn't notice that Misty often lies down behind the willow tree. That was it. Her beloved horse had to be where she'd left her a month before.

The rest of the day dragged on as her thoughts continually returned to Misty. She'd been dreading going home, but now she couldn't wait. When they arrived back from the market, Hope explained to Jessie's parents that she needed to return home straight away in case Misty had escaped.

'You know you're welcome here anytime.' Wyatt and Prue waved her off after they both gave her a bear hug.

Jessie drove Hope home and dropped her off at the gate. 'Thank for everything.' Hope embraced Jessie, almost crying. 'I'll let you know the outcome later this evening.'

Jessie pulled out of the drive tooting as she drove up the road. Hope's feet were heavy with reluctance as she dragged them up the front steps and flung open the door.

Her mother stood in the kitchen peeling potatoes.

'I'm back,' Hope muttered as she shot straight past Myra and headed towards her bedroom. She offloaded her backpack and rushed back out of the house.

Misty! She has to put her eyes on her horse. The paddock can't really be empty. She just can't fathom it.

She grabbed her bicycle and sped off to where the horse grazed. Her mother's voice chased her as she yelled, 'Wait, Hope—we need to talk.'

She continued cycling as fast as she could, a fifteen-minute ride to the paddock that felt like an eternity.

Misty was Hope's sweetheart. The noble, white Anglo-Arab mare was her best friend and the type of horse that was highly sought after in equestrian circles. During the difficult years at home when Hope felt as if she was invisible, Misty would provide her with solace. The horse always met her at the gate, waiting for her to hand her a carrot for a treat.

But this time, Misty didn't approach the gate as Hope sped down the track towards her paddock, calling her name.

Hope gasped for breath. She cycled like a lunatic, almost toppling off. Her cheeks burned. She imagined them tomato red as she swiped away the beads of salty perspiration that stung her eyes. She ignored the fire in her belly and jumped off her bike, throwing it aside. Her legs kept pumping, propelling her to the fence.

'Misty,' she yelled. The paddock was empty. She clambered over the wire fence, not bothering to open the wooden gate and caught her leg on some wire. Blood ran down her leg. 'Stupid fence,' she bellowed. 'Misty, please come. Where are you?'

She scanned the field of long grass. Her beloved companion was nowhere to be found. Misty was gone. But she couldn't have disappeared on her own. Somebody must have taken her.

Hope dropped to the ground, tears streaming down her cheeks. She wailed. Had the ground swallowed her? If it hadn't, she wished it would. 'Who would do this?' She cried.

Normally, she'd run to Joel who used to work part-time in the carpentry shop next to the paddock when he wasn't training horses. But eighteen months ago he'd left his job and disappeared from the Bay of Plenty.

Hope hauled herself up and trudged to the tack shed. It was empty too. The well-oiled saddle, bridle, and grooming kit were all missing. Even the horse float had gone. Her knees buckled, a flood of tears wet the ground beneath her feet. It felt as if a rock dropped into the pit of her stomach. She shook from head to toe. How would she get through this?

No answers came to mind as she fell back on the grass. Dark clouds above matched the ones in her mind.

Chapter Two

The tyres on the bike were almost flat, slowing her down as she
tore down the street towards her house. Panting, her heart in her
mouth, she rushed into the kitchen. Her mother stood aside,
wiping her hands on her apron.

'Where is she? What have you done with Misty? She's not in
her paddock. I said I'd come back for her.' Her legs shook like
jelly. She was sure her heart had missed a beat. The strain was
too much.

Her mother leaned over the stove, about to put a roast in the
oven and stopped abruptly. Hope stomped through the door and
glared at her. Her face muscles taut, she swiped her wringing wet
fringe from her eyes.

Myra put one hand on the bench to steady herself. 'I'm sorry,
Hope. We decided to sell her.'

Hope burst into tears. She formed a fist and banged it down on
the dining table then looked straight at her.

'What? What do you mean? You can't— she's mine. You had no
right!'

'After you left here for so long, your father and I thought it was
the right thing to do. You can't exercise her if you are out

"

gallivanting around. And the horse is just a distraction when you
go nursing.'

Why can't her mother just accept that she is not going
nursing? 'Just stop it! I'm not gallivanting around. I'll be looking
for work. And stop calling Frank my father. I haven't called him
my father ever since I found out the truth. You had no right to do
this behind my back. I hate you!'

'Don't talk like that. He's been your guardian all these years.'

'What! For the few times that he's been sober. And all this time
you still haven't told me the truth. Anyway— what have you done
with Misty?'

'She's gone to someone who'll take her to horse shows and
hunts, just like you.'

'Where— where has she gone?'

'The South Island. To someone who wants to enter her in
events. You don't need to know more than that.'

Hope collapsed back into the hard wooden chair. She leaned
her head on crossed arms on the table briefly. She wanted so
much for this scene to just be a bad dream. Soon she would
awaken and her life would be back to how it used to be. Abruptly
she sat bolt upright with renewed ardour, pushing the chair away.

'Why down south— so far away? You could have sold her
locally!'

'It was someone who wanted a white Anglo-Arab like Misty,
her breed and her capabilities. They'll take good care of her, I
promise.'

Hope thought she would never trust her mother again, let
alone believe her promises.

'I'm going to find her. And I already warned you I would move
out completely if you continue to withhold the truth about my

father from me. I'm an adult and can take care of myself. I'm leaving!'

Hope wilted. She was nauseated with the powerlessness over losing her beloved Misty. She sloped off to her room and stared at the ribbons and trophies she had won with the mare. Crashing on her bed she howled like a baby then lay on her back emotionally exhausted.

How could she be so cruel? I'll never forgive her.

She wanted to go back to see Jessie and tell her what had happened but it was dark outside. She was afraid to bike in the dark and had run out of energy. She knew that Jessie would be upset too. They had been riding companions for years. Hope was grateful that Jessie was home from university for the holidays.

She lay on her bed upsetting herself with pessimistic thoughts about the kind of bad things that might happen to her precious horse. This latest betrayal was for Hope the last straw.

Myra and Frank were stretched out on their worn-out couch watching television sharing a bar of chocolate. Hope crept into the hall so as not to alert them, and picked up the telephone.

'Jessie! I'm glad you picked up the phone.' Her throat seemed to have closed up as she choked on the words. 'It's Misty ... Sally was right, she's gone! Mum sold her!'

There was silence on the other end of the line, except for the sound of Hope sobbing into the phone. 'Please Jessie—can you come and pick me up again. I'm so angry with my mother. I can't stay here any longer.'

Having been given a car for her nineteenth birthday so that she could get to and fro to her university, Jessie had previously told Hope to let her know if she ever needed a ride anywhere.

'Sure, no problem. That's pretty mean of your mother. I'll leave now. I guess you can stay as long as you like. I'll talk to Mum and Dad.'

Hope scurried around, grabbing as much clothing as she could pack into a backpack, including all her photos of Misty. She walked into the lounge to inform Myra and Frank that she was leaving for good. They just sat there, speechless for the first time. Hope had grown up. Myra sat with her face in her hands looking totally bewildered.

***

Hope's home life had always been tumultuous. Frank's drinking had got out of control and there were increasing arguments between him and Myra. Hope's bedroom was off the dining room. When he walked in drunk each night, Hope was kept awake by her mother's yelling at him. This time, she had had enough.

Jessie's family were completely different to her own. They were kind and respectful towards each and they were also people of faith.

Jessie pulled up outside the house, tooting the horn a few times. As Hope opened the door and ran towards the car, Jessie saw the lounge curtain being drawn aside and Myra standing at the window her eyes shooting daggers at them.

'Quick, let's get out of here before she comes out to start a drama.' Hope daren't turn her head as Jessie drove off.

'Are you sure your folks don't mind me coming back again. I'll work for your father until I find a job.'

'It's alright, they know that. Dad has plenty for you to do. Anyway … you can ride one of our horses while you're here and we can go on a few treks.'

22

Once again, Jessie's parents welcomed Hope back as one of the family. It made her feel secure. But she felt drained. Her neck and shoulders ached from the emotional tension. She excused herself early that evening as her body longed for sleep.

That night, the house fell silent as the full moon lit up Hope's room like a searchlight. The light-weight curtains were no match for this moon. Hope pulled back the soft white sheets. The unusual pillowcases with Swiss embroidered edging welcomed her head, heavy from the pent-up emotion that plagued her. She lay still, listening to the sound of a cow crying out for its calf. *Hurry up Mum* she wanted to call out.

She imagined what life could have been like if she had a family like Jessie's. She was going to make sure she made the most of it … at least for now, she decided.

She awakened the next morning to the sound of a rooster crowing from the top of the hen house opposite Hope's room. The Border collie working dog ran around outside yelping.

There was a knock at her door. 'Are you awake, Hope? Mum's cooking breakfast. A special one for you.'

She tumbled out of bed, still half asleep, her shoulders aching from the stress of the last few days and opened the door to Jessie who was already dressed.

'That's sweet of her. She shouldn't go to any trouble.'

'Take advantage of it. Believe me, it might not happen again for a while.'

'Oh, okay, I'm quite hungry now. I'll just jump in the shower and be there shortly.'

Jessie was waiting in the dining room when Hope walked in with her long, voluminous black hair, still wet from the shower.

'I thought perhaps we could go over some of your plans to find Misty. If there's any way I can help, I will. Come—let's eat first, I'm famished.'

Jessie directed her to a French farmhouse style dining table set with old-fashioned Wedgewood crockery placed neatly around the table on place-mats.

Hope listened intently to the healthy communication going on at the dining table, pleasant conversations between Jessie, her parents, and her brother. She loved the way they involved her in their dialogues which made her feel part of the family.

Breakfast was over quickly, as Wyatt, Jessie's father had a busy schedule on the farm that morning.

'Here, you girls— grab a tea-towel each. After that, I think Wyatt wants to show you the jobs he has lined up for you, Hope.' Prue placed fresh tea-towels on the bench in front of them.

'You don't have to start the jobs today,' Wyatt interjected. 'Start tomorrow. I'll give you lassies the day off so you can help sort Hope out, Jessie.' He winked affectionately at his daughter.

'Great! Come on, Hope. Let's saddle up and take off to the beach. Twinkle, the horse you'll be riding, loves the water.'

***

They arrived at the beach not far from Jessie's home and took the horses into the sea on the incoming tide. Twinkle was half rearing with exhilaration. Suddenly he plunged forward. 'Hey! Whoa!' Hope kept her balance and tried to pull his head up, as the feisty gelding seemed to be sinking in the sand. 'Jessie, help me! I think we're sinking.' She screamed.

Jessie was further up ahead and had taken her own horse through a deeper part of the estuary where it was less muddy. She

turned her horse around and hurried back towards Hope. She
stopped a few metres away.

'Wait! I have a rope on my saddle. I'll try to pull you out. I can't
come any closer though.'

Jessie threw Hope the long rope, which had a large clip at the
end of it.

'Wrap the rope around Twinkle's neck then attach the clip to
the ring on your saddle.'

Hope followed Jessie's instructions. 'I'm ready. What now?'
She's done this before, Hope thought.

'Here— give me your reins. Just hang on tight. I'm going to try
and pull you out.'

Hope held her breath. Her body went rigid. 'I hope we don't
sink any further,' she shrieked.

'Don't panic. I've done this before.' Jessie leaned forward to
speak into her horse's ear. Now then Rusty— you have to pull
very hard.'

Rusty pricked up his ears as she nudged his sides with her
heels. He swayed back and forth as if to find his footing then
lurched forward, grunting as he heaved. Suddenly Twinkle gave a
loud whinny and forged forward, following Rusty out of the hole.

Hope shook. A large shot of adrenaline raced furiously
through her body like an electric current. 'I'm feeling wrecked. I
need a break!'

They rode up onto a large patch of grass along the foreshore.
Hope flung herself off her muddy horse, although she'd almost
fallen off him in shock. Her legs trembled. She found a small
hand-towel in her saddlebag and clumsily trudged to the
foreshore to soak it in the incoming tide. She began to wipe the
mud from Twinkle's coat with the wet towel.

'Poor boy. I'm so sorry Twinkle to get you into this. I'll give you a good warm wash down when we get back.' She wrapped her arms around Twinkle's neck and squeezed it tight.

'Whew! That was close.' Jessie gave her a sheepish look.

'You may have saved our lives, Jessie. How strange that the ground just went from under us. I've never been in quicksand before.'

'I'm sorry Hope. I am so used to coming this way with riding companions who are familiar with the area. I just didn't think that you wouldn't have known.' Jessie's voice quavered.

Hope turned and looked straight at her, eyebrows raised.

'You mean you knew it was boggy before I went in there?'

'I should have warned you. It's not real quicksand, just boggy in parts. It's okay if you know where to go. It happened to another friend in the past. I just forgot to let you know. I'm so sorry— please forgive me.'

'It's okay. You're forgiven, I suppose. I'm safe now. I won't come this way again though. I can assure you. Let's eat.' Hope could already see that her friend's fair complexion that usually resembled that of a porcelain doll had turned a strawberry colour.

She pulled her packed lunch out of her saddlebag and dumped herself on the grass. She gulped down the cold drink that Jessie's mother had packed for her.

'I'm feeling shattered. I wonder how my Misty would have reacted. Twinkle was very calm in spite of the danger.'

'He's a lovely boy. Sure-footed. We'll have to give them a good wash when we get back. Look— I have an idea. What about saving some money from your jobs and hire a truck to bring Misty back up here when you find her.'

'No. I won't be able to bring her back. Mum's put our paddock put up for grazing.'

'Really? Don't worry. We can graze her on our farm with my horses. Dad won't mind. I'll ask him.'

'You seem to be quite confident that I'll find her.'

'You will I'm sure.' Jessie's long slender fingers stroked the back of her hand.

'I'm going to pray that you do. You could hire a car and tour around for a while. There are those free relocation vehicles that have to be dropped off in towns with airports.'

'Yeah, I might take a look at that.'

'You could visit the local Pony Clubs and make enquiries about Misty. Take some photos with you to show the riders.'

'That's a great idea!' Hope's face lit up.

'I wonder if the new owner will keep her name the same.'

'Mum says that he said he would— but I don't know if I can trust her anymore.' Hope frowned.

'I suppose we'd better start getting back. I don't like the look of the dark clouds up there.' Jessie pointed upwards. They packed their lunchboxes back into their saddlebags and untied the horses.

Hope didn't say anything during the ride back to the farm. She let Jessie ride ahead while troublesome thoughts were living rent-free in her head. *What will Misty be doing right now? Who is with her?*

Chapter Three

After six weeks of working on the farm, Hope had saved up enough money for the airfare to Christchurch. Wyatt had paid her well and she'd worked from daylight to dusk. They didn't even charge her for her lodgings.

'Let's check your plans.' Jessie picked up Hope's papers and looked at the itinerary in front of her.

'Where are you staying in Christchurch? You haven't written it on here.'

'I don't want to stop there. I'll just keep driving towards Queenstown and if I get tired, I'll find a holiday park or backpackers for the night.'

Hope noticed Jessie was acting overly concerned as she sat obsessively looking over her itinerary several times.

'I've booked a relocation station wagon from the airport. I have to drop it off at Queenstown Airport in four days' time then I'll take public transport or hire another car from there. I'll need to find more work so I can afford to buy Misty back.'

'You said your Uncle Joel has a sister in Geraldine. Perhaps you could find her. Didn't you say that his family came from around there somewhere?'

'Yes, perhaps he's living there now.'

'How will you find out?'

'His sister will be in the phone book, I guess. I'll pay her a visit. Surely she must know where he lives. He's the only one who might be able to help me find Misty.'

'Well, looks like you're all set for your big adventure. Promise you'll write the minute you arrive in Queenstown. I'm going to miss you terribly. Dad's going to run you to the bus terminal so you can get the Road Services bus to Auckland International Airport.'

Jessie threw her arms around Hope, teardrops rolling down her pink cheeks. 'I'll say goodbye now as I have to feed the calves tomorrow and need to stay back here. I'm going to really miss you.'

'Pity you can't come and keep me company at the airport as I'll have a four-hour wait for my flight. I'll miss you too, Jessie. I don't know what I would have done without your help. I would probably be stuck at home depressed. Thanks so much.'

As Jessie stood in the doorway, Hope grabbed her and hugged her tight and then walked towards her room.

Jessie looked back, hesitating. 'Don't be upset, please. You can come up for the holidays sometime and stay at my flat. Anyway, you're going to be busy searching for Misty. Just keep the letters coming ... okay? I'm off to bed now. If things don't work out in the South Island, you could always come and stay with me.'

***

During her short flight on the DC-10 plane to Christchurch, Hope had been trying to solve a problem in her mind. Something just didn't sit right about Joel taking off in a hurry for no reason.

And according to her mother, he had gone to the South Island and she wouldn't tell her where. Why was everyone so secretive?

The airline stewardess with the soft voice interrupted her thoughts.

'Excuse me dear, but we'll be landing soon. Please fasten your seatbelt. Can I offer you a lolly?'

'Um ... Oh, it's okay, thanks.'

'It helps to stop your ears from blocking up.' The old woman sitting next to Hope nudged her as she unwrapped her own lolly.

With that, Hope quickly put her hand out for a sweet before the stewardess walked on down the aisle.

'Thank you,' she said to the woman. 'I think we're about to land ... I hate this part.' She squeezed both armrests tight.

'Me too. I just close my eyes and hope for the best.' The woman placed her hand on hers and smiled.

'Do you live here in Christchurch?'

'No, I'm on my way to Queenstown. I've quite a bit of travelling to do yet.'

'You poor dear. How are you getting there? Is someone waiting to take you?'

'No. I've ordered one of those relocation vehicles which I can have for four days. I have to drop it off at Queenstown airport. They are free except for petrol.'

'Sounds lovely dear. Look— you can drive by my house first if you like. It's near here, and I can give you something to eat and a cup of tea if you want. I was going to get a taxi but if I ride with you I can show you how to get there.'

Hope was thinking that the old lady was just looking for a ride home from the airport. She told Hope that she had been away for a few days visiting a new grandchild in Auckland.

'I don't mind giving you a ride home, then I would like to get on my way as I want to make good mileage before it gets dark. Thanks for the offer though.'

At the arrival gate at the airport, Hope saw a large placard, waving in the air with her name on it.

HOPE PETERSEN – SOUTHERN RENTALS

She collected her backpack from the carousel and walked to the exit gate towards the man in a suit who was holding the placard and waved at him. He put his hand up and hurried over to help her with her luggage.

'Do you mind waiting a moment? I promised a lift to an old lady who sat next to me on the plane. She lives near here. I'll just help her with her luggage.'

'No worries, madam. As long as she doesn't take too long. I have another job after this. Our office is just down the road so you'll have to drop me off first and sign the paperwork.'

'Hold on— here she is.'

The woman trundled slowly towards them, pushing a trolley.

'So sorry to keep you both waiting. Elsie's my name.'

The man in the suit helped them both load their luggage into the vehicle. After the paperwork was completed, Hope dropped Elsie home. The woman gave her a bar of chocolate and waved her on her way.

***

The station wagon was a spacious one, big enough for a large family and Hope found it easy to handle as she had driven one once before. She'd been warned by the rental company about black ice on the roads and not to take corners too fast, especially if it was windy.

Before she set off on her intrepid journey along one of the most scenic routes in New Zealand, she stopped to study her map. She'd a general idea of where she was headed but wanted to make sure she didn't get onto the wrong highway, as the thought of getting lost in the South Island was daunting for her.

***

The station wagon was comfortable to drive except that Hope became quickly fatigued from the intense concentration of driving in the wind. The vehicle roared along the highway until it started veering to the left and right as she struggled to keep it on a straight path in the strong southerly wind. She wished she had someone with her to take turns driving, but it wasn't going to happen. She'd have to harden up.

She was relieved when she saw a large green road sign that said "Geraldine" and slowed her pace. Pulling into a rest area just out of town she spotted a dairy. She pulled over and went into the store ask the shopkeeper if she could take a look at the local phone directory.

'Here she is! 'Nelly Grey. Primrose Avenue number 11.' She quickly jotted the details down.

'Thanks so much. I just hope she's there, that's all.' She waved to the shopkeeper as she walked out the door.

The man behind the counter called back to her. 'You can use my phone to call her if you like.'

Hope hesitated as if she wanted to walk back into the shop then changed her mind. 'No, thank you. I'll just drop by and see if she is in.'

She decided to chance it. If Nelly wasn't home, she'd keep going through to Lake Tekapo and stop at the camping ground there.

32

She parked the car outside an old, freshly painted villa. It was typical of a home of someone Nelly's age. An ornately adorned wire archway covered with deep pink, climbing roses provided a welcome feature at the front gate. As Hope walked into the entrance of the property, she noticed the pull-up windows were open and to the left of the home, white cotton sheets blowing in the southerly breeze.

'Can I help you, dear?' An elderly woman caught sight of Hope and popped her head out of the window.

Hope's eyes darted to and fro to see where the voice came from. 'Oh, sorry— I wasn't sure if anyone was home. Are you Nelly ... Nelly Grey?'

'Yes— yes, I am. Wait. Come around to the front door will you, dear.'

Hope scurried around the front, holding up a small bunch of flowers she'd purchased from a roadside kiosk and pushed them in front of Nelly's nose.

'I'm Hope ... Hope Petersen'. She handed Nelly the half-wilted flowers.

'They're lovely, thank you. Oh, my goodness. You've grown up. I haven't seen you since you were about ten years old. Come on in, dear.'

Nelly sat Hope down in a cosy floral armchair while she hurried into the kitchen and returned with a cold drink.

'Would you like one of my oat biscuits? I baked them last night. They're nice and crispy with a little ginger. You can take a few with you on your journey. Now tell me where you're headed.'

Hope took a handful of the biscuits, wrapped them in her paper napkin, and slid them inside her bag.

'Actually, I'm here for a reason. I'm trying to locate Uncle Joel. My mother said he's living in the South Island somewhere. He just up and left suddenly a few years ago and I don't understand why. But I need to ask him something important. I thought he may be around here somewhere, near his old hometown.'

'Oh, yes. My elusive brother— he did stay here for a short time after he left your home. Since he moved south, I see him less than when he lived up north with your family.'

'Do you know where he is? I need to find him urgently.'

'Goodness. That sounds serious— somewhere near Queenstown, I think. I can't remember what he said.' Her brows knitted in a frown. 'I can't remember if he said it was Wanaka or Queenstown.'

She let out a deep sigh. 'Sorry, Lass, my memory's almost gone. He said he'd purchased a piece of land and runs horses on it— trains them he said. But to be perfectly honest, that's all I know. In fact, I can't do much travelling nowadays. I had his phone number somewhere, but it's a toll call and I can't afford it.'

She rummaged through a drawer in her kitchen, looking for her address book.

'It should be in this book,' she mumbled, her forehead puckering as she realised the number was incorrect.

'Sorry, dear, I only have his old number. Perhaps he might be in the phone directory. I'll just take a look.'

Hope's heart sank. She'd driven all that way for nothing. Joel was her only hope of finding Misty.

Nelly handed her the book as she looked up and saw that Hope's face had dropped.

'I can't see his name in the main phone directory. Perhaps you'd better take a look yourself. Your eyes will be better than mine.'

It was futile. Hope's attempt at trying to track Joel down through Nelly had failed. Where to now?

'I'm so sorry to have put you to all this trouble, Nelly. I'll go to the public library in Queenstown and look through the phone directories there. But I really have to get on the road before it gets dark.' She jangled her keys and picked up her bag.

'Of course, my dear. It's no trouble at all. But I don't like the idea of a young girl like you travelling so far by yourself. You're welcome to stay here the night if you like.'

'I'm nearly nineteen, so not so much of a girl. That's kind of you, but I wouldn't want to put you to any trouble.'

'No, really. I welcome the company and I see you've turned into a lovely young woman.' Nelly quickly corrected herself. 'Are you going to Queenstown tomorrow?'

'No, I want to see the alpine lakes and stay in Wanaka. Maybe I'll get to see Mount Cook from there and take some photos then I'll head down to Queenstown after that.'

'Why not let me make you a nice hot dinner and then you get a good night's sleep before your big trip tomorrow.'

'That's so kind of you, I really appreciate it.'

'It gets a bit lonely in these parts. I'm grateful for the company.'

Nelly lit the fire and started singing. Hope could see that she was happy to have a guest for the night. The woman brought out a crock pot with a hot lamb casserole and placed it on the dining table.

'Now you sit yourself down here and tuck into this. I have apple crumble and custard to follow.'

When the meal was over, Hope wanted to find out more about Uncle Joel. She scanned the row of black and white photos in frames that skirted the oak hutch dresser and spotted a younger version of Joel.

'Do you mind telling me a little about Uncle Joel and his family life?'

'Of course. I'd love to.' She walked to her cabinet and pulled out a small photo album.

'You know Joel was born here in Geraldine where he spent his youth on my father's farm, hoping one day to take it over from him. While he was on active service during the last World War, Joel's American wife ran off with an English pilot and it took him years to get over a broken heart.

'Oh—I didn't know. That's terrible, poor man.'

'Then our father died of a heart attack on the farm while Joel was still overseas ... a double whammy. Mum and I had to put the farm up for sale. Dad had bequeathed the farm to Mum, Joel and me equally.'

'It's a pity he wasn't able to take over the farm. He would have loved that.' Hope picked up a photo of Joel riding a horse.

'When Joel returned from the war, he had to face the fact that his dream of managing the farm had ended. Mother had moved to Bethlehem to be near her relatives and Joel moved in with her.'

'That's when he met my family. You didn't go with them, Nelly?'

'No. I had good friends here and didn't want to move. I worked as a journalist for a firm in Christchurch by correspondence and bought this little cottage with the money from the estate.'

The sad talk about Uncle Joel's past bereavements drained Hope.

'Thanks so much for the delicious food and for talking to me about Uncle Joel. I'm tired now and need to get some sleep.'

As Hope was about to get into bed, the ageing spinster stood at the door to say goodnight.

'I promise I'll write down Joel's phone number if he rings me after you've gone. You keep in touch with me every now and then, if you can, and I'll let you know if I hear from him. Get some sleep now and don't worry, you'll find him.'

***

Chapter Four

'Thanks for the cooked breakfast.' Hope reached out and hugged Nelly as though they were old friends.

'Here's a little something for your journey.' Nelly handed her a basket full of home baking. A delicious aroma wafted out through the tea-towel that covered it. 'You don't need to return the basket. I have two of them.'

Hope was eager to start her journey. She only had four days left before the car was due back. It was a comfortable trip from Geraldine along State Highway 79 until she missed the turnoff at Fairlie junction for State Highway 8 to Lake Tekapo. She had to turn around and drive back to the junction, about fifteen minutes out of her way, which annoyed her. She pulled in at Fairlie for a quick break when she spotted a tearoom where she could ask directions for the turnoff to Lake Tekapo.

After travelling along State Highway 8, she started to feel weary, as she hadn't slept well at Nelly's house worrying about how to find Joel. She knew that tiredness was risky when driving long distances and decided to stop when she got to Lake Tekapo.

When she arrived at the lakefront she couldn't believe her eyes. The view was breathtaking. An abundance of pink and purple lupins formed a technicolour carpet on the lake shore which appeared like a stunning tapestry from a distance.

As she drove closer to the shore, she saw the renowned Church of the Good Shepherd, the quaint stone church framed by the famous Southern Alps.

She stood on the foreshore taking photos, not forgetting the lovely bronze statue of the collie dog, representative of the honoured sheep dogs of the Mackenzie country. Hunger pangs gnawed at her as she eagerly headed over to the tearooms. She hesitated, as she abhorred crowded cafes. Although this one was full of tourists, she battled her way along the queue to the food cabinet. She headed towards a small corner table and devoured her meat pie, one of her dietary weaknesses.

The starchy pie made her sleepy. She climbed into the car, after putting the seats down for a power nap. She set her clock for thirty minutes later as she was reluctant to pass through the mountains in the dark.

The alarm startled her. She'd been in a deep sleep and awoke to a raw chill that penetrated her. She quickly climbed into the driver's seat and started the engine to warm herself. She was grateful there was heating in the vehicle. She reached over to the passenger seat to pick up the map she had marked clearly.

'Mmm ... where are we? Oh, right here. I'm headed for the Lindis Pass then on to the backpackers in Wanaka. This route is long and desolate like most alpine passages, I'd best get through it in daylight', she mumbled to herself while an onlooker in the car next to her stared as she continued talking to herself.

The road along the Lindis Pass was long and windy, and dangerous in places because of the narrow, deceptive bends. The prolific clumps of brown tussock grass and expansive, brown, stark hills became monotonous and her eyelids were heavy. Although sleepy from boredom, she didn't want to stop and get out of the car as she knew she was vulnerable, a girl in a remote area alone. She opened all the windows and turned the radio up.

The car wound its way up the long windy pass towards the summit arriving at the lookout point. There before her was the awesome sight of the Southern Alps with a thin coating of fresh snow which glistened in the last rays before the sun disappeared behind the hills.

The temptation to get out of the car and take photos of the majestic mountainous view was too great. She looked at the rugged landscape surrounding her, and all she could see for miles was wide open spaces with brown tussock and bare hills with no vehicles in sight.

She put on her fleecy-lined bomber jacket and got out of the car, placing her car keys on the vehicle's roof while she pulled her new merino beanie over her ears.

The sleet had made the ground slippery. She opened the rear hatch and pulled out a pair of suede boots with rubber soles and as she fastened them, she glanced up. The view took her breath away.

She stood for a few minutes taking a short video of the snow-capped Southern Alps providing an artist's background to the expanse of brown rolling hills that reached for miles. She realised that once the sun faded, the alpine pass could be treacherous, and she quickly and cautiously walked back to the car.

As she approached the vehicle she caught sight of a large green parrot-like bird circling her car. It spread its wings, hovered over the vehicle momentarily, and landed on the roof. As she tentatively edged herself closer she noticed there was something in its beak, a sparkling metal object, and to her horror, the bird had picked up the car keys.

As she walked towards it she could see that it was a kea, a bird often seen in this location. She also knew that they are drawn to anything shiny.

'Hey! Drop it!' Instead, the bird spread its wings like an eagle, revealing a myriad of rainbow-like colours and took flight. Hope froze then her sense of horror intensified as she had fleeting thoughts of being stranded miles from anywhere as dusk was about to descend. For an instant, she wished she knew how to pray like Jessie and if her dear friend was with her, she would be praying for her right now. Deep inside, she heard her own spirit cry out silently, 'Help me, God!'

The bird darted sideways, encircling a log in a field over the fence near her parked car. It appeared to be fascinated with its new toy and to Hope's relief it appeared unable to grip the bulky keys in its beak. It just sat on the log jangling them, tossing them to and fro.

Hope clambered over the wire fence with difficulty, as there was no stile in sight. This was her last chance at retrieving her lifeline.

She crept up to the bird slowly. It must have been accustomed to being around tourists, as her advances did not frighten it. The bird continued to toss the keys about.

'Shoo, confounded bird! Let go of my keys— let go!' She charged at it, stumbling, muttering a quick prayer.

The creature glared at her, squawked defiantly while dropping the keys, and flew high into the sky. She rifled through the rough tussock grass to see where they had dropped and spotted them shining in the sunlight.

'Thank you, God! She sat sprawled on the log crying and quite shaken up. This escapade had thwarted her endeavour to reach Wanaka before dark.

The landscape through the Lindis Valley was in autumn splendour with trees covered in yellow and orange leaves. A sign that summer was drawing to an end.

The road appeared to go on forever and seemed to lead to nowhere. Again she regretted taking this trip alone and began to feel lost and isolated. Then, to her relief, she saw a truck in the distance, a huge petrol tanker. Another vehicle appeared approaching from the opposite direction again, and then it was still.

She nibbled at some of the biscuits Nelly had given her, and as she looked around for a ladies' restroom, she found there was none in sight. She knew she had to wait until she came out the other side of the Lindis Valley at Tarras. When she arrived there she didn't waste any time pulling in at Tarra's restroom and then did she not stop again until she arrived in Wanaka.

***

The Wanaka Backpacker's sign was a welcome sight as the car rumbled into the small township.

'Mmm— I could die for some hot chips,' she muttered, looking for a takeaway shop before they closed. She spotted one near the backpackers, ordered a meal, and sat by the lake eating her chips as she watched the sun go down. She opened the car window to listen to the unusual night sounds of the bird life, revelling in the peace. From where she was sitting, she could see the bright lights of the backpackers. Glancing at her watch, she started the car and hurried off to book in.

42

After a well-earned sleep, she woke just in time for the light breakfast she had paid for.

'Where are you off to today, Mount Cook?' The woman behind the reception desk came out from behind her computer. 'The weather has changed and there's a chill in the air so make sure you've plenty of warm clothing.'

'No, I'm heading to Queenstown to drop off my relocation vehicle, unfortunately. I'd love to go up onto the mountain but there's no time. But thanks, anyway.'

'Which route are you taking? The road through Cromwell, or the Crown Ranges which is a more scenic route.'

'I've been told the Crown Range is much more interesting and the views are better.'

'That's right, as long as you don't mind heights as it's scary in parts where it's steep. Just be careful on that windy road in case of ice.'

'Yes, I've been told about the dangers of icy roads. I use to go up Mount Ruapehu with my friend, Jessie. She was allowed to use one of her father's cars and we took a few friends up there. Sometimes she'd let me drive after I got my own driving licence. It was unnerving sometimes, but I got used to going up there in the car with chains.'

Hope wished she could have slept in longer as she was weary after the long trip through the alpine pass and the distressing episode with the kea bird.

There was something important she knew she had to do before leaving Wanaka. Try to locate Uncle Joel.

She walked back up to the woman at the reception desk. 'Excuse me ... I need to get hold of a local phone directory, please. Do you have one I could look at?' The woman with the horn-rimmed glasses looked her up and down. 'Can I help you perhaps, dear? I know a lot of people in this area.'

'Um ... I don't exactly know what area he lives in. I just know that he may live near Wanaka somewhere.'

'That's a bit vague ... who is it you're looking for?'

'His name's Joel Grey. He's my uncle.'

'Ah, let me think ... no, sorry, I don't know anyone around here called Grey. Are you sure he lives around here? I think I just about know everyone and there's been no one around here with that name.'

Her heart sank. 'It doesn't matter,' she mumbled in a low voice. I'll look in the library directories when I get to Queenstown.' She walked towards the door like a scolded dog with its tail between its legs.

'I think I may be able to help you— Joel Grey, did you say?' The farmer placed the cartons of free-range eggs on the reception desk.

'He was a good mate of mine when he used to live around here. Didn't come into town much. Gone further south I think. He did some work for me on my farm up there on the ridge.' He pointed towards the hills. 'He said he wanted his own piece of land. Said he had some special plan in mind but didn't say what it was.'

'Do you know where he lives now?' Hope thought she was on the brink of a breakthrough.

The expectant look on Hope's face appeared obvious to the man. 'Sorry, he didn't say as he didn't know himself at the time except that he wanted to go down the line to look around Lake Wakatipu for some acreage. He told me he wasn't much of a letter writer so I haven't heard from him since he left.'

'Oh, I see. I'll try to track him down around there when I arrive. Thanks anyway. I have to get on my way now.'

Things were looking up for Hope. Now at least she knew to start looking around Lake Wakatipu, though she knew the area was expansive. She sat in the car perusing the map again.

'Um ... let me see. I'll stop somewhere halfway, perhaps in Cromwell where all the yummy stone fruit is for sale.'

It was a clear, crisp autumn day, not a cloud in sight. Leaving Wanaka, she filled the car with petrol and drove along the highway trying to enjoy the enchanting surroundings without obsessing about Misty's whereabouts and the likelihood of finding her. She tried not to think about what she would do if she couldn't find Joel. But he just has to be somewhere near Lake Wakatipu. If she was Jessie, she'd be praying and asking for God's guidance. Perhaps that's what she needs to do now. She prayed loud and clear, in the same fashion that Jessie used to do when either of them had got themselves into trouble.

'Please, God! I don't know where to start looking. Uncle Joel seems my only hope of finding Misty. If you could help me find my horse, I promise I'll always believe in you.'

She started plea bargaining with God. She was desperate, hoping that he was the loving and merciful God that Jessie knew.

Chapter Five

The clear, crisp days were a change from the humid weather that Hope had experienced up north all summer. She wasn't used to snowy conditions with treacherous windy roads with ice. She heeded the advice of several people at the backpackers to drive carefully even in autumn. But to her relief, there was no ice on the road.

As she drove along the highway heading towards Cromwell, she became euphoric from the magnificent sight of Mount Pisa while passing through the scenic area.

Approaching the Clutha River, she spotted a jetty with a parking area nearby. She pulled in and parked where she could sit and look at the sweeping views of the large stretch of land opposite the river. The riverbank boasted trees covered with autumn leaves of, bright orange, red, yellow, crimson, and gold.

Her back hurt from sitting behind the wheel so long. She wished she could stop for longer to soak up the changing autumn scenery, but her desire to get to Queenstown to look for Joel was greater.

Near the parking area was a small tearoom where she was able to get a cream bun and a small mince pie to take on her journey, along with a bottle of cold Fanta.

She walked up to a tour bus driver sitting outside puffing on a cigarette, to get some directions.

'Excuse me— I'm heading down to Queenstown. How far is it from here please?'

'It should take around an hour to get to the centre of town.'

'Good. That's not too far then. Thanks very much.'

'Better be careful going through the Kawarau Gorge. There's pea soup fog up there right now and the road is treacherous. Take it slowly.'

A shiver went through Hope at the thought of driving in the dangerous conditions. It was bad enough driving through the Lewis Pass on her own and now this. She began to think she'd made a foolish decision taking this route. Perhaps she should've taken the less scenic, boring route from Dunedin up through the middle of the island. But she'd been looking forward to this trip with some of the most picturesque scenery she'd ever seen.

To her delight, the fog had started to lift. It was only at its worst at the beginning of the Gibbston Highway. There was even regular traffic along that road which made her feel more secure. After she'd driven at a snail's pace for most of the journey, hemmed in by a Kingswood station-wagon pulling a caravan, she pulled over on the side of the road to take a few more photos of the autumn splendour that had monopolised the trip.

As she drove towards the end of the highway, she noticed the large billboard stating Welcome to Queenstown Lakes District and breathed a sigh of relief that, although it had been spectacular, the long lonely drive was over.

She had to get the rental car back the next day, she remembered. Where to now? She didn't even have a place to stay.

She put her head out the window and asked a pedestrian where the Youth Hostel was. She found it easier to be told than to keep looking up everything on her roadmap.

'Not far from here, Miss … it's down by the lake.'

The man, who appeared to be a local, gave her clear directions to the hostel which was only a ten-minute drive away.

The large prominent, cedar building was the largest Youth Hostel she had ever seen and appeared super modern. It had a vacancy sign in front and all Hope wanted to do was sleep. The drive through the gorge had taken it out of her.

She parked outside in the visitor parking area and wearily dragged her heavy backpack through the hostel door, tripping on the doorstep.

'Whoops! Do you need a hand there? That's a big pack you're carrying.' The woman behind the front desk, moved towards her to help.

'No, I'm fine thanks. I've just been driving a long distance and need a break. Can I book in, please? I have a current Hostel membership.'

'Sure thing. Pat's my name. If you could just fill out this form here, I'll see which room might suit you. You can either share with others in the women's dorm, which will keep the price down, or pay more for a single room.'

'I'll have to sleep in the dorm as my funds are getting low.'

'Well, you're in luck right now. There's just one other girl in there who is from Sweden and nobody else has made a booking.'

Hope looked up from the form, struggling to remember some details. 'That's great. I'm trying to find my membership card. It's in my backpack somewhere, sorry!' She started opening all the backpack's pockets.

'Don't worry, just tell me your full name and address and pay me for the first night. When you find your card, you can give it to me later.'

Pat led her along the corridor to a pleasant room with six double bunks. She put her backpack on the floor next to a bottom bunk near the window which let a lot of light in. The blue and white cotton curtains looked fresh and fairly new. In the corner stood two large wooden dressers with lots of drawers, to Hope's delight.

As she unpacked the rest of her belongings and hung her clothes in the wardrobe, the other guest walked in and welcomed her. Hope was surprised to find she spoke good English.

'Nice to meet you,' said Hope, as she rummaged in her backpack for her flannel and towel. She rinsed her flannel in the basin in the corner of the room and started washing her face to freshen up.

'Did you come from far today?' The Swedish girl spoke good English to Hope's amazement.

'Not too far. I drove from Wanaka but the road was windy and there was thick fog at the beginning of the Kawarau Gorge so I had to drive slowly in case there was ice on the road. Now I just want to sleep for a bit.'

'I understand. Hey ... my name's Helga. I'm from Stockholm in Sweden. If you like, I can show you the lakeside after your nap. It's very beautiful down there and lots to see. Did you come here to go sight-seeing?'

'Hope's my name. I love the sights. The South Island is beautiful. I am from up north and have come to search for my show horse. My mother sold her to someone down here and I am trying to locate my uncle. He may be here in Queenstown and I think he might know my horse's whereabouts.'

'Really! That sounds serious. Does your mother not know where your horse's new owner lives?'

'Yes, I think so ... but she won't tell me. She doesn't want me riding her anymore. Look—it's quite complicated. I'll tell you later when we go for a walk.' Hope was careful about not divulging too much of her personal business to this stranger, although the woman appeared to be sincere. Perhaps she is someone with whom she can share her burden. She appears old enough to be her aunt or big sister. A problem shared is a problem halved, so the saying goes.

When she awoke, the curtains had been pulled across blocking the sun, which Hope gathered Helga had kindly done.

Her new-found friend crept quietly into the room. 'You were dead to the world. Must have been exhausted. Do you feel like a walk soon?'

Hope yawned loudly and peered out the window, squinting from the strong sunlight as she opened the curtains. 'Looks nice out there. What a clear blue sky. Yes, a walk along the lakeside would be great. I'll grab my camera.'

As they arrived at the lakeside, the steamship TSS Earnslaw had just pulled into the wharf and started unloading its passengers.

'Wow, look at that! Isn't it gorgeous? I love old boats. I wonder how much a cruise like that costs.'

'Let's go and see— the ticket office is over there.' Helga pointed to the building with a long queue of people standing waiting to make bookings.

'I don't think I want to stand in a queue like that. Let's take a look at that billboard over there.'

Hope pulled on Helga's arm directing her towards the signage while Helga hurried along, trying to keep up with the exuberant young woman who appeared to be full of life. But little did Helga know that underneath the bubbly façade, was a young woman with a broken heart in more ways than one.

'Oh no, look at those prices. I don't think I should be spending that kind of money. My funds are getting low.' Hope put her wallet back into her shoulder bag.

'Look … I have enough money for both of us. Please let me buy you a ticket.' Helga touched her arm and looked her in the eye.

Hope was far too proud to take this stranger's money. She did have funds in the bank and enough cash in her bag, but she knew if she started splurging it on tourist attractions it would run out. She realised quickly she had to get a job.

'That's really kind of you but I can't accept this right now. I'll come with you another day. What I need to do is look for some casual work.'

'What … today? You've only just arrived!'

'No, very soon though. First of all, I need to return my rental car back to the office tomorrow morning. It has cost me nothing except for petrol, as it was a relocation vehicle. I might have enough money to hire a small car while I'm job hunting. That's if it doesn't take me too long to get work.'

'Goodness! Queenstown Lake District is a huge place to try to get around if you have no car. I hope you find work soon.'

'Me too. I heard there's a lot of casual work on the farms around here. That's what I'm used to. I hope to do an Agricultural Science Diploma specialising in horse health. But I've chosen to take a year off to find my missing horse and get some money together.'

As they wandered along the path around the lakeside, Hope went mad with her camera. She was overawed by the sight of the Remarkables, the mountain range covered with snow, even in autumn. The sun glistened on the peaks which made them even more spectacular. The TSS Earnslaw steamship had started up and chugged its way across the lake towards Walter Peak Station full of passengers again. Hope wished she could have been on it but she was a diligent budgeter and knew her funds could only go so far, particularly if she decided to buy a little car.

Nelly had shown Hope an album with photographs of Queenstown the night she stayed with her, and she remembered the photos of Walter Peak Station and Lake Whakatipu.

Perhaps she could find work over there on one of the sheep stations around the lake. She was in a little world of her own imagining finding a job with horses on a sheep or cattle station. Helga startled her suddenly by tugging her arm and brought her swiftly back to reality.

'Sorry, Hope. We're at the end of the walkway. How about we go back and at least let me buy you a hot roll at that kiosk.'

'That's nice, thanks. Would you like to come with me into town to return the car? If I can rent one from there, I'd like to go to the car yards and look for a cheapie to buy. I've been saving up for months for one. When I get a job that pays well, I can swap it for a better one.'

Helga hesitated. 'Sure ... I'll come. Where do we start?'

'I've made a list of some car yards— here, look.' She handed her the piece of paper.

'Why don't we pick up some hot rolls at the kiosk and go and sit where we can talk.'

The girls purchased their food and milkshakes. By the time they'd eaten, they had all their plans mapped out.

Chapter Six

Hope woke to another clear fine day. The sunshine was not as warm as it had been as snow flurries had fallen during the night on the Alps.

After a hasty breakfast, Helga was waiting for her at the front door of the lodge as planned. 'I hope you have plenty of thermals on today. There's been a cold snap, and it'll get colder with that southerly wind blowing.' Helga clucked over Hope who found her over-protectiveness irritating as it reminded her of her mother's behaviour.

I suppose she means well. I should be grateful that she's looking out for me, I suppose.

When she dropped the vehicle off at the car rental office, she explained to the salesman that she was needing a cheap rental vehicle to use so she had some wheels to go hunting for a vehicle to purchase.

'You say you just want to buy something cheap and you don't mind how old it is? I think I've just the thing for you here to save you going to the car yards.'

'What do you mean? I thought you just rent cars, not sell them.'

'Ah ... but we have another string to our bow. We've ex-rental vehicles that we sell at a low price. Most of them have done over a hundred thousand miles but they last forever.'

'What kind of cars?'

'Come over here, lassie and I'll show you.'

Hope was surprised when she followed him to the back of the building to find a long fleet of used cars in tidy condition.

'Take your pick. Any idea what model you're after?'

'I've been told the Toyota Corollas are the most reliable. Do you have any?'

'Funny you should ask. We just added this one to the stock this week. I'd say it would be just what you're looking for. If you take this you won't have to rent one or go looking to buy one. It could take you days to find one if you don't know your way around.'

Hope turned to Helga. 'What do you think? Do you know anything about them?'

'Yes, I do. My father had one a little bigger than this. He told me they are reliable and the engines last forever. I'd go for this one Hope, honestly, I would.'

They took their time inspecting the mustard coloured car and were both impressed.

'Wow! Beautiful upholstery. Looking at it, you wouldn't think it's an ex-rental. It's been well preserved.'

'Yes, you're sure right about that. We look after our cars, as we know how they can depreciate in value. Well, what do you want to do, ladies?'

'Is there a warranty on this car?' Helga asked, as though she was experienced in car buying.

'Yep. Three years, or if you pay a bit more— five years.'

Helga looked at Hope. 'I think you should take it.'

'How about a hundred dollars off if we pay cash today?' Helga was used to bargaining in her own country.

The salesman hesitated, looked at the car papers, and studied the girls momentarily.

'I suppose it sounds like a done deal. Come into the office and I'll sort out your insurance if you want that now too.'

***

Hope drove into a tree studded glade alongside the lake and turned on the car radio.

'Well, my girl. You're now the proud owner of a very nice car. And you won't get lost in this one. I've never seen a mustard coloured Corolla before. You'll have to give it a name.' Helga passed her a bag of potato crisps. 'Do you think we should be eating these in your tidy new car, Hope?'

'I don't think it matters as long as we don't wipe our greasy hands on the upholstery. I've some moist wipes I keep in my bag. I know—Sunflower! I'll call it Sunflower!' They both laughed.

'Where do you go from here? It's a good thing we both booked out of the hostel and you don't need to go back to get your luggage.' Hope was ready for a new adventure.

Helga took Hope's hand. 'I'm sorry Hope, but I'm headed for Milford Sound. I've some time to kill and would appreciate a ride to the bus station where I'll store my luggage in a locker. I'll walk around the town for a bit until my bus is due in.'

'I'm going to the Post Office to look up the directory for my uncle's address. I can drop you off first.'

'I've really enjoyed hanging out with you though. It's been an inspiration hearing about your great road trip adventure.'

They found a coffee bar in town and then went their separate ways after swapping addresses. Hope was disappointed she wasn't able to give Helga a stable address, as she didn't know where she would be in the near future.

After Helga walked off in the opposite direction, Hope started to realise how she needed a buddy and how much she missed her closest friend Jessie now that she was alone again.

She thought she'd better get in touch with her parents and stopped at the nearest stationer's shop for writing material and postcards. As she entered the Post Office she remembered she'd redirected her mail to Post Restante and walked to the counter to request it.

'Here you are, Hope. Looks like there's a bit of mail for you.'

To Hope's surprise, there were some letters. One lengthy one from her mother, one from Doug, and two from Jessie.

'Thanks so much. Um ... do you know if there's a camping ground near the lake anywhere? I was hoping to get my tent up.'

The lady looked her up and down. 'Camping, you say? Surely it's too cold for that now. There's snow on the Alps. But if you insist, there's a good Holiday Park about two miles south of here if you follow the lake around. It's opposite the Golf Club. They have cabins too if you change your mind about the tent.'

'I have a mountaineer's tent, an alpine sleeping bag, and all the thermal clothing. My brother used to take me camping in the National Park and we were warm as toast with snow on the summit.'

'Rather you than me. They also have a hot spa pool if you need to thaw out.'

'Not in this weather. I think I'll give that one a miss.'

'Here are the directories you asked for. I hope you find what you want.'

She sat down and waded through the phone books, not knowing where to start. There were four of them and she scanned each one for Joel's name and address then slumped back in her chair, despairing.

This is hopeless. This is her last chance at finding some clue as to Misty's whereabouts. What is she to do now?

She gathered the heavy directories and slapped them back on the counter.

'Thanks very much. I've finished with them.'

'Found what you were looking for?'

Hope turned to look at the woman whose face appeared kind. 'Well—no. I can't find the person's name anywhere.'

'Maybe I can help. Who is it you're looking for?'

'My Uncle Joel—Joel Grey. Apparently, he purchased a block of land around Lake Whakatipu somewhere and I need to see him about something important. I've driven down from Christchurch where I flew in from Auckland.'

'That was a big trip you made. Grey, you say. Mmm ... sorry dear, I haven't heard of any Greys around here. What does he do?'

'He breaks in horses and trains them. He also does a bit of farm labouring.'

'Have you come all the way down here just to look for him? Couldn't your parents tell you where he is?'

'It's a long story. Sorry to bother you. I'll get on now.' Hope grabbed her bag and sloped out the door despondently. Again, she didn't feel like telling this perfect stranger all her private business.

'Wait! Wait a minute—perhaps I can help you.' The woman appeared hot and flustered running after Hope. 'I have a spare room in my modest little abode not far from here. I often take students from the Bible College nearby but the room is free at present and they're all on a long break.'

'Oh, that's kind of you, but I really enjoy camping and the great outdoors. It's like being on one big adventure. Thanks, but I'll be fine.'

The woman wrote some details on a piece of paper and handed it to her. 'Here is my name, address and phone number. Grace is my name, Grace Rogers, but you can call me Gracie. Please phone me or drop by if you need anything, anything at all.'

'Thanks, but I'll be okay once I find work. I'll probably stay on here in Queenstown until I track down my uncle.'

'There plenty of work in hospitality if you like waitressing or hotel work.'

'No thanks. I'm looking for farm work, preferably with horses.'

The woman ducked under the counter then stood up handing her a business card.

'Here is the name of a high country station owner who picks up his mail from here. In fact, I know him quite well as his daughter went to the Bible College here and I gave her a room for a while. Jock Weston is his name.'

'Where's his station? I don't know the area that well.'

'It's just out of Kingston at the southern part of the lake. I hear he takes on casual workers and I've sent some of the Bible students to him for work. If you like, I can give him a call and let him know you might be in touch.'

'Um ... I suppose that will be okay but I can't promise I'll phone him.'

Hope didn't want anyone to take over her life after she'd managed to escape her mother's control. She changed her mind quickly.

'Sorry— but I'd rather you didn't phone him. I have his card and if I decide that it's right for me to approach him, I will. I really appreciate your help though.'

Hope was aware she was disappointing Gracie though she knew she had to keep her boundaries.

'Promise I'll be in touch if I need help. Bye for now. I'll see you next time I collect my mail.'

***

Hope thanked the woman and drove in search of the camping ground. As she drove around the lake, Aspen Holiday Park appeared and to her relief, a vacancy sign.

She trundled into the office and rang the bell then leaned on the counter and glanced at the brochures in front of her.

'Hello there. Sorry, I was out back. Have you been waiting long?' Hope averted her eyes as an over-weight man with his belly cascading over his belt waddled in behind the counter. He wiped his mouth as though he had been eating.

'No, not really. Do you have any vacancies?'

'Depends on how many nights you want to stay.'

'I'm not sure yet. I have to find some casual work so it might take a while. Perhaps a few nights to start with. What's my cheapest option?'

The man looked her up and down as if he was trying to work out if she was a person of means or not then spotted the old car.

'We have basic cabins for twenty dollars a night or tourist flats which are a lot dearer. That's if you aren't thinking of camping, which of course is the cheaper option. One night will be ten dollars. I'll show you the cabins if you like.'

'Um … no thanks, I'll take a tent site. I hear it won't be snowing for another month, only on the mountain peaks. I have plenty of warm gear.'

The manager led her through the camp to her tent site shaking his head as if she was mad. She chose a spot near a family who were just settling in opposite her which made her feel a little more secure.

'Kitchen and shower block are just over there.' He handed her a small bottle of milk. 'We have basic supplies in our office and apart from that there is a shop just along the road and Minimart in town.'

'Thanks for that. Okay if I park here?' She pointed to an area next to the tent site.

'Of course, as long as it doesn't encroach on the next tent site if anyone arrives.' The man hobbled off, scuffing the dusty ground in his rubber Jandals back to the office.

Hope looked around to check out her neighbours. There was the family opposite her who appeared to have well-behaved, older children. They were about fifteen metres away from her tent, which was situated next to a paddock full of sheep. To the left and right of her, the tent sites were unoccupied but further along the row was a young couple who waved and smiled at her. She did not feel so alone.

She hastily dragged her gear out of the boot of her car and commenced to erect her igloo-shaped tent. As tiredness set in, she couldn't remember how to erect the tent poles.

'Can I give you a hand? My kids have the same tents and I'm used to putting them up.'

The middle-aged man from across the way grinned jovially at her and picked up one of the poles.

'Oh, you don't have to. I'm sure I'll eventually work it out. It's just that it's been a while, that's all.'

Hope turned slightly, staring at the pole in her hands so that the man would not see the warm flush spreading up her neck. Within minutes, the tent was up and she expressed her heartfelt gratitude.

'Why don't you come and join us for supper. I think we're playing cards tonight.'

'Ah … thanks very much but I'm pretty tired. I think I'll shoot along to the fish and chip shop up the road then turn in. Perhaps another evening.'

She zoomed off in her car and sat by the lake eating fish and chips, wondering where all this was going to end. When she'd finished, she cleaned her hands using the wipes she kept in her car then pulled out her mail she'd been keen to read.

The first letter she opened was from her mother who admonished her for taking off to the South Island and upsetting her. Then Myra's tone softened when she started to emotionally blackmail Hope about going home to start a "real" career. She went on to say that she needed Hope there, as Frank was ailing and she couldn't manage all the tomato picking on her own. The local teen who'd been working for them had left.

'There you go— that's why you need me to come home. Typical!' Hope spewed out her frustration at her mother's guilt-trip.

She read the rest of the letter which left her cold. No mention of her Uncle Joel, Doug, Misty or anything or anyone she held dear. Her mother knew she was grieving over these losses but showed no compassion.

Hope quickly stuffed the letter into the glovebox of the car and started on the next letter. It was from Doug and she knew this one would give her some degree of comfort

Dear Sis

I have just arrived home and heard from Mum about your incredible intrepid journey down south. Please let us know if you are safe. You can send a telegram. Mum is a nervous wreck, though I know she caused you grief by selling Misty behind your back. She said you took off down south to find her. Have you tracked her down yet? Where are you, Sis?

I have moved back to Bethlehem and decided to stay at home for a while to help Mum out with the tomato picking. She said she had insisted you come home to help out too now that Dad is ailing, but you don't need to do that. I know you want to have a gap year before you start university. Jessie told me about that when she was in town on her break. She sends her love and has already written to you.

I think it will be good to work and save money before you start your studies. I am enclosing a cheque for you, a belated birthday present which is some of the superannuation I received from the army. Sorry I was not around for your birthday. I hope this will make up for it. I want you to use it to tide you over until you get a job. And promise me that you will get straight on the first flight home if your luck runs out!

I forgot to tell you. I have been seeing a counsellor at the local Anglican Church near my flat in Auckland who has helped me

deal with my flashbacks. I think I'm getting well, Hope. He is a Pastor and has been giving me spiritual help too.

Thinking of you

Lots of love
Doug.

Chapter Seven

It was starting to get dark and the sun had disappeared over the Remarkables while Hope sat in the car reading the mail. She cried after reading Doug's letter.

She decided to read Jessie's news when she gets back to her tent where she can read with her lantern. She started to get cold and hurried back to the camping ground.

As she pulled in, she noticed the tall pine trees about the camp were swaying in the wind. The weather had changed, but she'd been reassured by the camp owner that there was no sign of rain, according to the weather forecast.

She gathered her torch and lantern and made her bed ready for the night. She wasn't keen on sleeping on the ground, but her tent was watertight and her airbed was comfortable. She'd inflated it before she'd set off for her takeaway meal.

She snuggled into her duck down sleeping bag zipping it up to her neck. A welcome rural odour emanated from the cow paddocks through the fence.

There was a full moon that illuminated the tent, as she lay still fascinated by the night sounds of owls and other birds settling in for the night. Then she started to think about the journey she'd made, such a long distance for a young woman alone. And for what? Nothing had worked out for her. No sign of Uncle Joel anywhere. He must be here somewhere. What will she do if she can't find work? Or what if her money runs out? Then she remembered the cheque for five hundred dollars she had in the envelope from Doug.

If her money runs out, she's not going home. She'll go and stay with Jessie in Palmerston North and find work there. Jessie said to start praying each night and she'd also be praying for her too. The more Hope prays the more she'll begin to trust God and her faith will increase, Jessie had told her.

She lay there trying to talk to God out loud.

'Please, God, I'm not very good at this as you already know. I've got myself into quite a pickle by landing down here with Uncle Joel nowhere to be found. No job and no place to go. I said that if you help me find Misty, I'll always follow you. I promise I will, but first I need to track down Uncle Joel. Please help me! Amen.'

She took out the small pocket Bible from her backpack that Jessie gave her the day she left. She opened it at a verse that her friend had highlighted for her ...

"Trust in the Lord with all your heart and lean not on your own understanding. In all your ways submit to him, and he will make your paths straight."

Suddenly a strong gust of wind shook the tent and startled her. The wind seemed to increase in force until she began to worry that her tent would blow away. She remembered that it was anchored to the ground sheet and her weight would stop it from going anywhere.

Then in the bright light of the moon, she saw large shadows towering over her, things that appeared like giants. She shuddered. The muscles between her ribs tensed so she could hardly breathe.

The strange figures began to sway back and forth until she realised they were the silhouettes of the tall pine trees along the fence-line. She lay there imagining they were huge angels sent to watch over her while she slept.

She recalled a story Jessie had told her about the archangel Michael and imagined him to be one of the figures standing over her tent protecting her. She drifted off to sleep.

***

The early morning sun woke her and streamed through the mesh window in her tent flap. She needed to go to the camp bathroom and reluctantly crawled out of a warm sleeping bag as the cold air bit her face when she unzipped the tent. She pulled on her fur-lined boots, donned a thick jumper over the track pants she slept in and stumbled over to the shower block, combing her fingers through her matted hair.

As she walked back to her tent, she saw the woman from the caravan opposite. She was standing outside in the crisp morning air in her pink pyjamas. She smiled and waved at Hope then disappeared back inside the caravan.

After visiting the camp bathroom, Hope scratched around in a hamper for the muesli and fruit she packed for breakfast. She mixed up a little milk powder with the water from her drink bottle. She tipped some coffee into a mug and wandered into the kitchen to get boiling water for a welcome hot drink.

'Are you heading off today?' a voice from behind.

67

It was the husband of the woman with pink pyjamas. He dumped a pile of dishes in the sink and started washing up.

'I'm not sure yet. It depends. I have to find work but I don't know where to start.'

'That's a real pity. Now I feel guilty going off skiing today. I hope you find something. Did you know there's an employment office in town? They have job vacancy listings in their window and might be able to help you.'

'That's really helpful, thank you. I'll try there first. I'm dying for a hot shower. Hope they are good ones.'

'They're really good, lots of pressure. Unlike some of the camps we've stayed at.' He trundled off to his caravan with the bucket of clean dishes.

Hope ate her breakfast in her tent then walked over to the utility block for a shower. She went back to her tent to look for her work resumes and references then drove her car into town to find the employment office.

She was astounded by the sight of the Remarkables at sunrise. Majestic, snow-capped peaks that appeared like pink and orange gelato ice-cream glistening under the dawn sunrays. In spite of the strong winds during the night, the morning sky was clear and not a cloud in sight.

As she entered the building, there was a long queue right up to the door. The young men stood staring at Hope, as she was the only young woman in the queue. After a long wait, her name was called.

'Hope Petersen— come with me please.'

As she followed an officious looking woman down the passageway, Hope's spirit fell and she did not feel in a secure position. She'd heard there was very little work in Queenstown for women except in retail which she abhorred but plenty of work for men on the farms.

Who's going to take on a girl Hope's age with all these great strapping young men waiting in line for farm work? She sneered at the queue and continued to torment herself, then sat down in front of the recruiter's desk.

'Good to meet you, Hope. I've had a look at the application form you've filled out and there's not much in the way of work experience listed. We can only offer you a position in retail or hospitality, which is the work we have available for women.'

'Oh! But I'm not interested in that kind of work.' The hairs on the back of her neck bristled.

'Well, I'm sorry. The only work left is for farmhands or ranchers, and there are plenty of young men available for that. It would be far too strenuous for a girl like you.'

'That's untrue. Didn't you read what I wrote on my resume about my farm experience? I can handle horses really well and have general farmhand experience.

'I'm sorry, but we're unable to offer you anything at this time. Perhaps come back in a month and see what's available then.'

'It's okay, I have some other options.'

The recruiter could see from the look on her client's face that there was no point in continuing the conversation. Hope roughly grabbed her documents and stormed out of the building. As soon as she was back in her car, she sobbed with exasperation.

What's she going to do now? No job, no leads on Misty or Uncle Joel, and only enough money to provide food and accommodation for a few weeks. She'll have to keep the money that Doug gave her in case she finds Misty and needs to buy her back from her owner.

She pulled out the business card that Gracie at the Post Office had given her and decided to phone the high country station manager. This may be her only chance.

She sped back to the camp, this time not taking as much care on the road as usual and almost knocked over a pedestrian.

As she entered the camp, she parked near the office and wandered inside to ask if she could use the phone.

'That'll be twenty cents. You can put it in that jar, thanks.' The camp owner went through to the back of the office to give her some privacy.

She managed to get hold of Jock, the station manager and came off the phone beaming. 'Thank you!' she called out to the camp owner. 'I've finished now.'

Things were starting to look up for her, as the farmer said he was short of staff and would be interested in giving her a trial. She couldn't believe her luck that he'd invited her to come for an interview that afternoon.

The road leading to the sheep station was bumpy and dusty. As she drove to the crest of the hill overlooking Corriedale Hills Station, she was amazed at what she saw. There must have been thousands of acres spread out for miles covered with sheep that appeared like tufts of cotton wool in the distance. The spectacle was something she'd never seen in her life before.

The road seemed to go for miles and eventually she arrived on time at the station. She approached the homestead down a long driveway lined with gold popular trees giving it a stately appearance. It was as though she was entering the Taj Mahal.

As she approached the colonial homestead, it reminded her of home with its billows of smoke escaping the chimney and the strong smell of macrocarpa wood burning. She also caught sight of a tall burly man and a well-built woman walking back from the barn to the house waving at her, showing her where to park. There were two vehicles— an old land rover and a truck parked in front of the house.

'You'll be alright over here, next to the Land Rover. Meet my wife Gilly— and you are Hope, isn't that right? I couldn't quite pick up your name over the phone.'

'Yes, that's right. Hope Petersen. Pleased to meet you.'

'Jock and Gilly Weston. Come and take a seat.'

She shook hands with them both and followed them inside.

'I've just made a pot of tea if you would like to join us.' Gilly went into the kitchen and brought back a tray and placed it on the table.

'Do you mind if we sit at the dining table? There's more room there for us to sit around. Just easier I suppose.' Jock pulled a seat out for Hope then quickly stoked up the Kent fire while she sat down and instantly relaxed.

'Can I pass you a lemon muffin? Just fresh this morning.' Gilly passed the plate around.

'Thank you ... how do you find time to do all this with such a large sheep station?' Hope assumed Gilly worked on the farm.

'We have a few station hands. There's also Hamish, our son who assists Jock, and our daughter Charity who helps out when she's back home between Mercy Ship missions.' Gilly went to the lounge and looked out the window.

'She should be home soon. She's on leave and just popped into town to go shopping.'

'What's the Mercy Mission?' Hope wondered if they were Christians like Jessie and her family. She'd remembered that

Gracie at the Post Office told her that Jock's daughter stayed with her when she went to Bible College.

'It's a hospital ship that provides free health care to people in desperate circumstances.' Gilly poured another cup of tea for Hope then one for herself.

'Jock just drinks coffee. I told him it will be the death of him one day, but he never listens.'

'What does Charity do on the boat?' Hope asked.

'She's a volunteer school teacher and comes home every four months. At least she's back home for six weeks between voyages.'

Jock looked agitated, as though he wanted to get to the reason for Hope being there. He darted a glance at Gilly.

'Well, Missy, what experience have you had with farm work. Any references? Jock sat there scrutinising her all of a sudden, while Hope pulled out some papers.

She showed him the inflated reference she received from Jessie's father and the proof of her acceptance into the university to study Agricultural Science. She also pulled out all the certificates and photos she had to prove that she was a proficient horse rider.

'Excellent. That's what we need. Someone who knows how to manage a stock horse. In this high country, you can't work without being able to ride. I've just the one for you. I'll take you over to see her a bit later. How about I give you a week's trial and if you're as good as you say you are I'll keep you as a casual worker. That's until our two station hands are back from the shearing competitions up north. How does that sound?'

'That sounds great, thanks. You mean ... as a volunteer for the week?' Hope's fine jaw set as if stressed. 'Except I need to find a proper paid job though.'

'Oh, for goodness sake, no! It's illegal for me to not pay you. I don't practice slave labour. Of course, I'll be paying you the going rate for a novice station hand, regardless if I keep you on after the trial. That's minus food and accommodation which leaves you a bit you can put aside for yourself.'

'Can I work overtime?'

'If you still have the energy. The work is hard and you'll be tired at the end of the day. Tomorrow we're docking the lambs' tails and that'll take it out of you. I'll get Charity to give you a quick rundown on it tonight.'

'You mean ... I'm hired! Have I got the job?' Jock melted when he saw her eyes almost popping out with delight.

'You don't think I can let you go after all those convincing testimonials you gave me. As long as you can handle the pace, you should go well. You'd better get back to the camp and pick up your things. You might just be back in time for dinner.'

***

Charity placed her shopping bags onto her bed. She wandered down the hallway and to meet the guest in the bedroom next door. As she approached Hope's room, she found her busy emptying out her backpack and placing her carefully folded articles of clothing in the drawers of the dresser provided.

'Hi, there! Welcome to Corriedale Hills Station. Mum said you'd just arrived. Charity's my name. Dad asked me to show you around the station before dinner. How does that sound?'

Hope was excited and couldn't wait to get onto the high country property which evoked a flood of nostalgia about working on Jessie's farm.

'Yes, sure. I'd love to. I'll just change into my jeans and jumper. I'll be there in a minute.'

'You'd better wear a warm jacket as it's pretty cold up here in the hills. The southerly wind bites.'

Charity went outside to wait for Hope and sat on a hay bale until she arrived.

They spent an hour walking around while Charity gave Hope the "grand tour". She showed her one of the mares she could ride and to Hope's astonishment, the horse was a white mare just like Misty, and although not an Anglo-Arab, she was beautiful in Hope's eyes. She was ecstatic. Now she knew she'd be happy at Corriedale Hills Station.

'Why don't we go and sit in the barn and chat before dinner. I'd like to hear all about your great adventure and why you've come all the way down here from the Bay of Plenty. You don't look much younger than I am. Dad said you're almost nineteen.'

'Yes, I am. What about you—how old are you?'

'Twenty-two.'

Hope thought, judging by the girl's maturity that she was older. She told her all about her search for Misty and her Uncle Joel, that he might be the only one who would have an idea of Misty's whereabouts. *Could Jock and his family help?*

Chapter Eight

After the first week of working the sheep on horse-back, Hope was exhausted but invigorated. She and Charity finished moving a paddock of sheep then they tied up their horses and stretched out in the sun and rested.

The wind was biting just as Charity had warned.

'I'm glad you told me to wear plenty of warm clothing. I'm wearing three layers of merino undergarments.'

She passed the thermos flask of coffee back to Charity. They both pulled out their packed lunch that Gilly had provided and talked at length about their lives.

When Hope told Charity the truth about her grudge against her mother including her extreme sadness at losing Misty, her confidant could see that she was holding back tears and handed her a clean handkerchief.

'Thanks, I feel silly now … but I'm desperate and don't know what to do. Look—this is Misty.' Hope passed her a small photo she'd removed from her jacket pocket.

'It may sound strange, but I think I've seen that mare somewhere at a show.' Charity took a closer look then handed it back.

'We don't see many white Anglo-Arabs around here at the local shows. But I was at one we had here recently when I returned from the Mercy Africa on leave. I entered the dressage event and noticed a distinctive white Arab mare that was getting ready to enter the show jumping event across from me. We rarely see an animal like that in these parts.'

'Who was riding her, do you remember?'

'A girl I think, younger than you. I can't quite recall, sorry.'

'That must be Misty, it has to be! How can I find out?' There must be a way.' Hope's voice sounded shaky. She cleared her throat.

'I suppose we could contact the show and ask for a copy of the program of events. The names of the competitors will be on it ... wait on—I think I still have one in my bedroom. Come on, we best be getting back. Dad needs us for the drenching this afternoon. I'll take a look after dinner.'

***

'Charity! Can you give me a hand to dish up the meal? And Hope, dear, would you mind setting the table?' Gilly took the lamb roast out of the oven and started carving it up while Hope took the cutlery into the dining room and started laying the table. Jock walked in.

'We need to have a chat later, Hope. I want to talk about your trial period and give you some feedback.' He had a bottle of Stout in his hand, flipped the lid off, and sat down at the dining table.

Hope realised she'd have to make up her mind. If she stayed on at Corriedale Hills, she'd have no time at all to search for Uncle Joel or Misty. And what if the horse that Charity saw really was Misty? She was perplexed and knew she needed to work although her wages and the money from Doug would keep her

76

going until she found another job. Perhaps Jock would keep her position open for a week while she went back to Queenstown to make enquiries about Joel.

'Come on— let's eat while it's hot.' Gilly had just poked her head around the kitchen door.

When they'd all finished the meal and gone to sit in the lounge, Jock invited Hope to join him in his office to discuss her trial period that had just ended. Hope sat holding the sides of the chair, feet crossed, and waiting for Jock to break the bad news.

'Well, Hope, we're all flabbergasted. To be honest, none of us believed that you'd be able to keep up with us all. Our station hand and Charity and I were amazed at your riding ability on the steep hills as well as your stamina. And you were like a torpedo when you were helping with docking and drenching the sheep. You could keep up with all of us.'

She pressed her hands to her cheeks as the usual pink colour suddenly returned to them.

'I can offer you a permanent position here if you'll take it.'

Although it was good news, Hope felt put on the spot. She knew she needed the money and this was a top job with a perfect family including accommodation, food, and horse. But she had to open her mouth now and beg Jock to employ her after a week's break. She needed time to follow up the lead on Misty.

She spewed it out and told him the whole story, including the lead she had from Charity. When she'd finished talking, Jock excused himself to go back into the lounge to discuss the situation with his wife and daughter.

'Hamish is back next week and so are our two part-time station hands who've been on holiday.'

Gilly untied her apron strings and wiped her hands. 'I think you should take Hope on after a week's time when she has finished her investigations. She is distraught over losing her horse.'

'Yes, I know. I've got a feeling I may have met that bloke Joel she's talking about. I could make some inquiries about him and make a phone call to Federated Farmers.' He walked back into the office and found Hope waiting with her head in her cupped hands.

'Hope, cheer up! We'd be more than happy to have you back here again in a week and I'll give you fulltime work. But it will initially be on a casual basis. That's in case you need more time off to sort this out further down the track.'

'I'm so grateful, thanks so much. If I find Misty, I'll have to have work to be able to afford to buy her back if the owner will agree. It might be at a high price.'

'I think I've met your uncle, Joel Grey, in fact, I think I was introduced to him at a Federated Farmers meeting earlier this year. He had a ranch somewhere outside of Queenstown but I can't remember where. Does he break horses in, do you know?'

'Yes, that's him. He broke in my horse, Misty. He's also a trainer. His sister in Geraldine said he bought some land down this way but no one seems to have heard of him and she doesn't know where he lives.'

'I can find out from the Federated Farmers. They have a list of names and addresses of members.'

'Oh, please will you? That'll be amazing if you can find him for me.'

'I'll do my best. Where will you stay if you leave here? You're welcome to stay on here while you're doing your search. Except we're a bit far away from everything, I suppose.'

'That's really kind of you, Jock. But it's best I stay in a backpackers or Youth Hostel in Queenstown as it may be more practical.'

'Well, I'll look forward to having you back here in a week. Pity you won't be able to meet Hamish before you go, but he will be here when you get back.'

'I might go and pack now. I have to make a list of places to go to make my inquiries.'

'I'll make a few phone calls tonight to try and help you. Don't give up hope of finding Misty. You'll get her back, don't worry.'

While Hope was busy filling her backpack, she couldn't stop herself from looking at her mini photo book of Misty and suddenly had a meltdown. She crumbled in a heap on her bed and sobbed. In desperation, she prayed 'Please, God, I'm at my wit's end. Please help me find her, I can't stand it anymore.'

There was a gentle knock at the door. Hope saw Charity standing in the doorway and she quickly wiped her eyes.

'Sorry ... Hope, are you alright? I knocked twice but you couldn't have heard me. Will you let me pray with you?'

Hope remembered Charity had been at Bible College. Jock gave thanks for the food at the table each night and Hope guessed they were all believers.

'Um ... if you like, thank you.'

That night, she slept peacefully for the first time since she'd arrived in Queenstown.

She awakened to the sound of Jock scolding one of the dogs for bringing a rabbit inside the house. She showered and dressed then joined the family at the dining table early.

'I've some news for you, young lady.' Jock took a piece of paper out of his shirt pocket. 'Good news, at that.' He handed the note to Hope. Her heart jumped as she held her breath and then her head spun.

'Oh, my goodness! You did it, you found Uncle Joel!' She looked at the note again. 'But there's no address or phone number. It just says Dart River Ranch, Glenorchy'. Her smile on her face quickly vanished as the corners of her mouth turned down.

'The Federated Farmers would not give out personal details for privacy reasons but just the name of his ranch is all you need. We can find that in the yellow pages directory.' Jock had already picked up the directory from the telephone table. He quickly flicked through the pages. 'Here we are … here's the phone number and the address of the ranch. What do you want to do? I'll write it down for you and you can phone him.' The smile returned to her face again.

In Jock's office, Hope's stomach churned as she picked up the phone. 'Can I speak to Joel Grey please?' A young male voice answered.

'Sorry, he's not here. He's out of town, and won't be back until tomorrow. Can I take a message?'

'No— no, thanks. What time do you expect him to be back tomorrow?'

'He should be back by midday unless he stops off somewhere else on the way.'

'I'll come tomorrow afternoon then.' Her heart raced with excited expectation.

'Well, what did he say?' Jock looked intensely at her.

'I spoke to a ranch hand who's looking after the stock while Uncle Joel's out of town. He said he's due back tomorrow so I'll go out there and find accommodation nearby.'

'Mmm ... Paradise. That's a remote farming valley about twenty kilometres north of Glenorchy village. It's right on the edge of Mt Aspiring National Park.'

'Sounds isolated to me. I suppose there's no accommodation out there.'

'I believe there's a large hostel at Lake Kinloch, about twenty minutes' drive from Paradise. It's supposed to be clean and popular with tourists.'

Charity came into the dining room to clear away the breakfast dishes.

'What am I hearing? It sounds like you've found him ... your uncle, I mean.'

'Yes, isn't it great? Your father's been a great help. I'm so grateful all of you for your support.'

'Well, you'd better get off and get out to that hostel and get settled. I think you might need this.' Gilly handed her a chilly bin full of provisions with ice packs to keep it cool.'

'Wow, you're so generous. I don't expect you to do this and you don't have to. I can manage, honest, I can.'

Jock quickly interjected. 'Just take it, lassie. It's the least we can do to help. And you play it safe. Drive carefully and give me a phone call before you come back so that I know what you decide to do.'

Hope drove off down the long driveway then onto the windy highway again, this time really believing that God had heard her prayers.

***

Hope found the drive to Lake Kinloch just as spectacular as the voyage through the Lewis Pass had been. She was overwhelmed by the breath-taking views and couldn't stop gaping at the abundance of forest and greenery all the way to the lake.

This is heaven. No wonder Uncle Joel wanted to live down here. Why did he just up and leave like that? I'll have to ask him what happened—that's if he'll tell me.

As she drove around the lake to Kinloch, she reminisced about the good old times spent with her uncle while she was growing up and pondered on her childhood memories of Joel breaking in Misty and going on the hunts with him.

The drive to the hostel took over an hour. She clutched the steering wheel tight as she drove carefully on the slippery roads. When she arrived at the hostel, to her delight it wasn't full. 'Great! An empty dorm.' She dumped her backpack on the bare mattress.

In the lounge, the warm glow from the old-fashioned stone fireplace caught her eye. She unpacked her provisions in the small kitchen and placed them in the allotted bag with her name on it then prepared a basic meal of rice risotto with bacon and fresh vegetables.

She went out onto the veranda after her meal, eating a banana for dessert. She was mesmerised by the colours of the electric blue lake and technicolour sunset.

A freshening breeze sent a chill through her. She headed back to the dorm and rested for a while on her unmade bunk, lying on top of her sleeping bag. Though she usually read a novel to relax, she was too tired to read the book she had packed.

An hour later, having woken from a short nap, she went back onto the veranda to look at the changing moods of the lake, dressed in her fleecy bomber jacket and lined trousers. When eventually darkness fell on the lake, she looked up at the sky and saw that it was the clearest she had ever seen, full of sparkling diamonds and shooting stars. It was so still except for the odd sound of an owl or migrating ducks overhead. 'Thank you, God, thank you for bringing me to this heavenly place,' she said quietly, then went indoors to the communal lounge to join a few of the tourists who sat around the fireplace.

Chapter Nine

It was a brisk southern morning and Hope was glad she packed extra thermals. No more sleeping in the tent for her now. She'd left her wristwatch in the bathroom. When she went back to look for it, she was surprised to find no one had stolen it. She's been so forgetful lately— it must be all the stress about finding Misty and Uncle Joel. 'Oh my goodness, it's eleven thirty already,' she uttered.

She rolled up the extra blanket that one of the night staff had given her during the night when she'd been woken by the cold. She'd not yet adjusted to the sudden drop in temperature. She handed the receptionist at the front desk the blanket.

'Thanks, it was a great help. Hope you don't mind but I need a few directions. I can't follow this map. Do you know how to get to Paradise, near Glenorchy please?' Hope handed her the map.

'Sure, I do. Let me take a look.' The receptionist put her glasses back on.

'Do you know where in Paradise you are headed?'

'A ranch on Glenorchy-Paradise Road. It's called Dart River Ranch. Do you know it?'

The girl laughed. 'We know everything and everyone around here. I went on a riding course there last year.'

'Oh, really? Do they have a lot of horses?'

'Yes, heaps. They run a lot of different activities. You can take your own horse there for some training or they'll provide one. They also run treks along the Dart River occasionally which I have done.'

'Sounds amazing. I can't wait to take a look.'

'There are a few hunky ranch hands who work there too.' The girl flashed her a smile and Hope didn't stop to think what the twinkle in her eyes meant.

That must have been one of the ranch hands I spoke to over the phone.

Hope loved the scenic drive to Glenorchy. When she arrived in the village she was surprised there were signs of civilisation. Apart from a pub and a small general store, there was also a school. She stopped to buy some food and sat in the car to eat it. She looked up and saw the sign for Glenorchy-Paradise Road. *At last, I might get a good lead to find Misty.*

She drove along Paradise-Glenorchy Road past Rees Station looking for the gate she was told about when suddenly she saw the sign DART RIVER RANCH with a prominent image of a black stallion. Tall pine trees loomed high, their branches almost shrouding the sign.

As Hope neared the old, colonial farmhouse that presented itself at the end of the long driveway, she held her breath in anticipation.

A young man appeared to be walking back from the stables near the house. He turned and waved then approached her vehicle as she pulled over and leaned out the window.

'You must be Hope— Cole's my name, Cole Digby. You can park here. Come on inside. Joel's been delayed but suggested I show you around the ranch if you're interested. He shouldn't be much longer. Would you like to come in for a coffee first?'

She couldn't help ogling the debonair young man. As she stepped out of the car he towered above her in his high boots and brown leather Bullhide hat with leather whip stitching around the top. She tried not to stare.

'Oh, thanks, I will. I'm a bit of a coffee addict.'

'Joel has one of those coffee filter machines and fresh coffee beans. Anyway, how do you know him?'

'He's my uncle.' She didn't want to get into the issue that he was probably just an uncle-like figure and not related. Just a close family friend.

'That's strange he never mentioned you. But, then again, he doesn't tell everyone his business. He's quite a private person.' Cole pulled out two well-worn bachelor mugs from the cupboard and opened a packet of biscuits.

'Gingernuts. Hope you like them.'

'My favourite, but usually when I can dunk them and I won't do that in company.' She gave him a sheepish grin.

'Do you live here?' She discreetly looked around at the sleek furnishings that were unlike the usual rugged interior of a high country farmer's abode.

'No, over there.' He nodded towards the large green paddock through the window. Hope spotted a small wooden bungalow she could see in the distance.

'Joel lives here alone. See that cottage over there.' He pointed at the home that Hope had already picked out.'

'That's for Joel's ranch hands and I'm the only one he has on the property at present. I'm in my final year at Otago University studying Agricultural Science.'

'Wow! That's unbelievable. I've been accepted for the Agricultural Science Diploma Equine there, also. It's just a one-year course full time or part-time by distance learning.'

'I majored in Equine Health as well. That's why I'm here with your uncle. He's been training me in horse breaking techniques and supports me with a horse breeding program I've started.' He poured the coffee into the mugs and passed her the biscuits. 'Anyway … When do you start your Diploma?'

'I'm having a gap year and wanting to save some money doing farm labouring, particularly working with horses. Next March I hope.'

They finished their coffee. 'Come outside and look around the ranch. Cole led her out to the back paddocks.

'We've bred some amazing horses with two of our stallions. They are real stunners, a white Arab stallion, and a black Kaimanawa beauty we brought down in the first muster two years ago. The mares and foals are kept in the stables during the cold months until the foals get stronger. I can show you them later.'

'What do you mean in the first muster? Where do you get the horses from?'

'Oh, of course, you don't know. They're the wild horses from the hills around Paradise.'

'I've never heard of wild horses around here. Are there many?'

'I don't think so. We discovered two small herds which you see in those two paddocks over there and we have broken in several of them. The stallions took a lot of work to get to the stage of handling them.'

'Do you do any show jumping or dressage with any of them?'

'Hold on— we'll go and bring the horses down to the front paddock for a feed. They won't hurt us. They're just frisky with all the spring grass.'

'I mean, do you show the horses?' Hope persisted.

'Yeah, we've just been in the local agricultural show recently and our best riders entered the events on our own horses. Wait on—if you could just stand aside while I open the gate to let them through.' He unlatched the long wooden gate.

'Perhaps you'd better stand behind the fence. We shift them into a different paddock each night to give the grass a rest, but some of them can wind each other up and start a kicking match trying to push through the gate.'

Hope stood back and observed how he gathered the horses together with skill and coaxed them through the gate. She leaned against the fence watching each horse trot past one by one then caught a fleeting glimpse of a white Anglo-Arab mare rushing by, which was partly shadowed by another larger horse on her side.

She looked again and froze with shock. She placed her hand on her stomach as the churning started, triggered by her distress.

'Misty! Misty!' She cried loudly.

Cole looked across at her as he moved towards the gate to close it. 'Are you alright? Why are you calling that name?'

Hope couldn't hear him. She started running towards the horses, tripping over piles of horse dung and stumbling on the uneven ground as she raced towards her mare.

'Slow down, Hope! You don't want to frighten them.' Cole was bewildered at her behaviour. He didn't understand why she was calling out that name, as it appeared she just went over to pat the horses. Then the distraught look on her face was obvious.

She quietly walked up to the herd. A few of them threw their heads in the air and trotted away from her while one white mare pricked its ears and turned towards her, slowly walking in her direction.

'Misty— it is you, I just knew it!' She wrapped her arms around the horse's neck and sobbed. Misty gently rubbed her head up and down Hope's back as if to comfort her.

Betrayed again! Why did her Uncle Joel do this without letting her know? He has a lot of explaining to do. She needed to stop and slow her breathing down. She clutched her chest then leaned against Misty's shoulder with her face buried in the horse's mane and started to relax.

Cole walked over to join her with a puzzled look on his face. Seeing her face wet with tears, he pulled out a clean handkerchief and awkwardly offered it to her.

'Here, it's a clean one. Sorry—I don't understand what's going on.'

She tried to compose herself, struggling to swallow then spoke with a husky voice, 'She's mine, that's my horse. Uncle Joel is the one who bought Misty. He's my friend, so why would he do that?'

She looked Misty over and could see she was in perfect health and appeared content.

'What's he doing with her? I mean, what's he using her for— to breed?'

'No, we have experienced riders who live in Queenstown who don't own their own horses and we allow them to use our show horses like Misty for jumping events and dressage. But most of them are at university and can only come here during their semester breaks, so Joel and I have to exercise the horses as best we can.'

'Oh, poor Misty. She must have been missing me.' She nestled her head into the horse's mane as the mare responded by nudging her and letting out a soft whinny.

'I'm going to confront Uncle Joel when he arrives and find out the truth. Why did he come all the way back to Bethlehem to bring Misty down here behind my back?' Her mood changed from one of deep sadness to anger.

As Cole shuffled back to the house with Hope, he kept his hands in his pockets and head hanging low. He didn't say a word, as though he was scared to upset her any further.

'Take a seat in the lounge and I'll see what the pot of stew is doing.'

Hope sat enjoying the aroma emanating from the kitchen that reminded her of her mother's cooking. Then she remembered why she was here.

A white Ute arrived out the front of the house. Joel came through the front door and threw off his boots.

'Are you there, Cole? Sorry, I'm so late. There was a car accident causing a traffic jam. I gather that bright yellow banana out there is Hope's car.'

Cole walked back out to the hallway to meet him and chuckled at his comment. 'Oh, yeah ... that's Sunflower.' He struggled to keep his composure.

'Sorry I was delayed, Mate. That mare I went to see seems to be ready for breaking in. The owners are trucking her down from Ashburton next week.'

Joel whispered something to him as he walked into the lounge where Hope was sitting. Cole followed after him. 'What a surprise to see you here!' Joel wiped beads of perspiration from his brow and gave a nervous cough.

'If you don't mind, I'd rather talk to you in private. I've just
seen Misty in the paddock out back and I want to know what
she's doing here.' Her demeanour was prickly.

Cole took the cue. 'Look, guys ... you two appear to have a lot of
catching up to do. I'll disappear back to my digs now and see you
tomorrow. Are you staying overnight, Hope?'

'I ... um— I don't know.'

'Yes, she is. You will stay, won't you? Please, Hope. I need
some time to explain why Misty is here and why I left your home
so abruptly when I did.'

'Well, I suppose I could. I'll have to phone my employer at
Corriedale Hills Station and tell Jock I've been delayed.'

'Use the phone in my office. It's not a toll call from here.' Cole
tied up his bootlaces and poked his head through the office door
where Hope was about to pick up the phone. 'I'll see you in the
morning then, Hope. Perhaps Joel will let me take you on a bit of
a trek around here on horseback and show you the Dart River.
They need exercise, anyway.'

'I'm not sure yet. Do you mind if I let you know in the morning
as I may not feel like doing anything.' The look on her face said it
all for Cole and he waved and walked off.

After her phone call to Jock at Corriedale Hills Station, she
wandered back into the lounge to find Joel kneeling down stoking
the fire. He scrambled to his feet.

'How did you get on?'

'Oh, he was quite amicable and said I can let him know when
I'm ready to start work.'

'Hope— why not hear me out while I tell you why I left under a
cloud. But be prepared for some unexpected news. After we've

talked, I'd like to give you a good hot meal. Cole has prepared a beef stew in the slow cooker that'll warm you up.'

Hope suspected he was trying to soften the blow as he handed her a mug of hot chocolate. They sat down in the lounge in front of the fire and Joel's old black cat spread itself out on the hearth mat. It rolled onto its back pulling up its front paws, trying to look cute.

Joel sniffed nervously and gave a cough to clear his throat. 'When you had the big quarrel with your mother and went to stay with Jessie on the farm for a month, I received a phone call from her. She was upset that you refused to stay at home and start a nursing career at the local hospital. She said that your horse-riding was a huge distraction from your studies if you were going nursing.'

He stooped down to stoke the fire and drank the rest of his hot drink then continued, 'She seemed obsessed about you going nursing and sounded as though she was determined to talk you into it.'

Hope bristled. 'She was more interested that I live the life that she missed out on and fulfil her fantasy of becoming a nurse!' She snapped.

The deep-seated resentment towards her mother rose again. *How could she be so selfish and scheming?*

'I think she was bitter about me gaining my independence when I went to work for Jessie's father on the farm.'

'The thing is Hope— she kind of coerced me into going up and transporting Misty in your horse float down here so I could take care of her. I didn't buy her. Your mother begged me to take her and made me promise not to change her name.' He sat in the chair wringing his hands and hesitated as if a bomb was about to explode.

'You mean you drove all the way from here to the Bay of Plenty just to take care of Misty. Mum's so mean— but what you did to save Misty from going to a stranger is unbelievable. Thank you!'

'I knew that if I didn't do it, your mother would carry out her threat to sell her, and who knows whom she might have ended up with. I planned to wait until you left home for good and then tell you the truth as I'm doing now. I knew I couldn't get in touch with you. Your mother wouldn't let me.'

Hope leapt up from her armchair and threw herself at Joel, wrapping her arms around his neck and kissing him on the cheek. She was overjoyed instead of being angry with him.

The phone rang in the office. 'Ah, no, not right now. They'll phone back if it's important.' He sauntered back into the lounge, rubbed his hands together and gave another one of his coughs.

'There is something else I need to clear up with you. I'm afraid I've another shattering confession to make.' He stammered as moisture appeared on his temples and started dripping down his face. He wiped it with a handkerchief from his pocket.

Hope jumped out of her seat and walked off to the bathroom. She wondered what on earth he was about to tell her. Perhaps he had cancer, or he was about to move. Or maybe there was something wrong with Misty. The phone rang again. She washed her hands and walked hastily back into the lounge. Joel wasn't there and she could hear that he was on the telephone. The office door was closed and there was only the sound of a muffled voice through the wall. It was a lengthy phone conversation and then he walked back to join Hope. 'So sorry I was so long, but it was your mother phoning.' I thought if I didn't answer the phone it would keep on ringing and thank God I picked it up.'

'What? What do you mean? How does she know your phone number?' Hope felt that this was all becoming a can of worms.

'It's a long story and I was going to tell you. It'll have to wait now. Unfortunately, your mother rang to tell me some bad news as I told her you were here. Your father has just died suddenly in his sleep.' He walked over to her armchair and placed his hand on her shoulder. 'I'm so sorry, Hope.'

She froze and sat in the chair looking like a stunned mullet. She wanted to tell Joel that she knew that Frank was not her father.

'How? Why— what's happened to him? I'd better phone her back.'

'No— she said not to. He's had a sudden massive heart attack and she's had a lot to deal with right now. Doug's with her and the Vicar is on his way around. But she wants you to go back for the funeral and I said that I'll fly back to Auckland with you. We can get a connecting flight to Tauranga from there.'

Hope couldn't believe her ears. Just when she'd become reunited with Misty and started making a new life for herself away from the unhappiness of home, misfortune struck. *Now I have to go back again.* Her heart sank.

'Poor Frank. I didn't even know he was ill.' She hoped he didn't suffer as she remembered what a kind man he had been in spite of being a drunkard.

'The doctor told your mother he wouldn't have suffered. He had not been obviously ill. It just happens to some people, apparently. His funeral is in two days. Your mother said we can both stay at your house. Why are you calling him Frank? You used to call him Dad.'

'Oh … no reason. I suppose it sounds modern.'

Joel appeared awkward all of a sudden as though he wanted to tell her something.

'But I won't stay on after the funeral. I have to take care of Misty now and make up for lost time with her.'

'I've been thinking about that too. What do you think about staying on here and working with me? I need help with the horses and I can train you to do the work I do. When you're at university, you can always come here for your holidays and you'll be on wages.'

Hope's mouth fell open. Suddenly her grim countenance changed to one of elation.

'Really! That would be fantastic. I'll be doing distance study but will have to go there for labs and workshops. But what will happen to Misty while I'm at university?'

'I can take good care of her just as I've already been doing. Cole has done some of his papers by distance study. You could ask him all about it.'

It was like a dream come true for Hope. She was much more focused on this amazing proposition from Joel than she was on the death of her stepfather. Perhaps when she tells Joel what Doug had told her about Frank not being her biological father, he might help her to find her real Dad. But she'll have to find the right moment to tell him all about it, and now is not the right time.

She sank deep into the armchair with the cat on her lap and the heat of the fire lighting up her face as well as her heart.

<h1 style="text-align:center">Chapter Ten</h1>

Doug stayed on after the funeral and helped his mother to prepare the market garden for sale with the help of one of their casual workers. Joel and Hope stayed for five days then returned to Paradise. As Hope had never experienced any close relationship or bonding with Frank, she did not grieve his loss. During his stay, Joel had detected there was still unnerving tension between Myra and her daughter who constantly bickered with each other.

Hope was relieved that Doug had decided to stay on and share the family home with his mother while he worked at the hospital, which took the pressure of Hope in that she didn't feel guilty about staying away.

'You know you're going to have to forgive your mother someday and the sooner the better,' said Joel, elbowing Hope as he drove to Paradise from Queenstown airport after they flew in.

'Why is that? I don't feel ready to forgive her. She doesn't deserve it and she has always kept secrets from me. Anyway, what were you and Mum having heavy discussions about? I saw you both in deep conversation after the funeral at the cemetery. And later at home too. Mum appeared really agitated.'

'We just had some unfinished business we had to take care of, that's all. Tying up loose ends when I left in a hurry. How about we discuss this as soon as we get back to the ranch.'

For the rest of the trip home, there was silence. Both of them struggling to assimilate the truth that was about to rear its irksome head.

***

Joel unloaded their luggage from the boot of his car. Hope dumped her bags on her bedroom floor and walked back to the kitchen where Joel had just put the kettle on.

'Well, you still haven't told me why you up and left all of a sudden. I remember you were going to tell me the night I arrived when we sat in front of the fire and Mum had rung to say that Frank had died.'

'I suppose I needed to wait for the right moment. I didn't know what state you'd be in after hearing of Frank's death.' Joel's voice sounded full of intrigue.

'I'm over Frank's passing already ... do you know that he's not my father?'

Those words hit Joel with a thud as though he'd been assaulted. He struggled to give a reply, as he was unprepared. He needed time to work out what to say and now she put him on the spot. He grabbed some coffee cups and walked into the lounge with Hope in tow.

'I ... I did know that. How did you find out?' He flopped into his well-worn armchair while Hope sat opposite.

'Doug told me ages ago. He said that when Frank was drunk one night when Mum and I had gone out, he spewed out this confession that he was not my father. He refused to tell Doug whom my real Dad was and made him swear that he would not

97

tell anyone. I think Doug knows who my father is, but he said that even if his suspicions were right, he would never tell me. Will you help me find him, Uncle Joel, please? I don't know where to start.' Her voice quivered.

Joel went to the kitchen and poured coffee. He brought it back in on a tray. She noticed a sudden pallor in his face that was not there earlier.

'You're having coffee?' He handed her a cup.

'Thanks.' She took the cup and tried to steady her hand as she placed it on the table next to her.

'It's a long story, Hope— I'm your real father.' He cringed as he said the words then sighed as though he was relieved at having let go of the emotional burden.

'What! First Misty, then this. No wonder my mother didn't want me to find you. Is she a party to all this deceit?' Hope didn't know whether to be happy or to start crying. After all these years, this was a dream come true for her. But it left her confused.

'I don't understand. My legal name is Petersen, not Grey.'

'Yes, I know. Frank agreed to put his name on your birth certificate to avoid a scandal.'

'But Mum was married to Frank, not to you!'

'I'll tell you all about it but you'll need to be patient and hear the whole story. Your mother has given her permission to tell you everything.'

He loosened his shirt collar by undoing his top button that revealed a red, moist neck. 'Do you want a biscuit with your coffee? I put some chocolate macaroons in the fridge.'

'Sure.' Her lips tightened and she sat staring in front of her.

'Won't be a minute.' He walked slowly to the fridge as if he was deliberately deferring the dreaded moment of truth.

He handed her the packet and sat back in his armchair, this time leaning forward on the edge of the seat with his arms on his knees and wringing his hands. He looked up at Hope who just sat glaring at him.

'Your mother and I met when we were young, about your age, and fell in love. My parents were not wealthy. They were an ordinary working-class family. My father was a stock auctioneer in Geraldine where he owned a farmlet.'

Hope's eyes stayed transfixed on his face.

'He had a heart condition and retired early then died soon after. My mother and I moved to Bethlehem as Mum wanted to be near her family. Your Aunt Nelly stayed in Geraldine where she had a good job and friends.'

'Where did you meet my mum?'

'I attended the local pony club and so did your mother. Once a month our farming community in Bethlehem held a dance, a great shindig in the local hall. Your mother and I loved dancing and would always pair up on those evenings and then we gradually started courting. I cycled miles to visit her at her home, in spite of her parent's disapproval. We decided that we would marry one day, but that was way in the future.'

'Why didn't you marry her?'

Joel rubbed the back of his neck, as if though Hope's questions had tensed his muscles.

'I desperately wanted to but her father was an influential man and convinced her she would end up as a no-hoper without any status or social standing.'

'Where does Frank come into it then?'

He wiped his brow with his handkerchief and continued.

'Well— so much for your mother's high social standing and status. She'd been coerced by her family into marrying Frank Petersen, a marriage of convenience ... a loveless organised marriage.'

Hope grimaced and compassion showed in her eyes.

'Well ... the money didn't come Frank's way and he and your mother struggled for years after the war. When he returned from active service in 1944, Frank began drinking heavily but prior to the war he hardly touched a drop.'

'Oh, that's really sad! I never knew,' croaked Hope, as Joel continued.

'Before Frank went off to war in 1942, Doug was born. He's your half-brother. Your mother suffered the misery of being left with their baby boy whilst trying to manage a market garden alone, with the occasional help of her parents. After the war, she became embittered by another hard blow. Frank confessed to her that he didn't love her and no longer sought an intimate relationship with her. His love affair was with the bottle. They slept in separate rooms for the whole of your life. Myra believed the war had caused the damage to their relationship, but I'm not sure about that.'

'Wow, that's right! Now I understand. I thought they didn't sleep in the same room because of Frank's drinking, but now it makes sense.' The reflux from Hope's stomach returned which she always experienced when upset. She swallowed the biting acid that swam in her throat. Then she felt a kind of relief at knowing the truth.

Joel continued, gingerly. 'He was a lot older than your mother and didn't keep good health which limited his ability to work. His parents virtually abandoned him because of alcohol abuse and threatened that if he didn't stop, they would disinherit him, which they eventually did.'

'So where do I come into it?'

'When my mother died in 1950, she and Frank invited me to have meals at their home. Myra had become a broken woman from the neglect and strain of living with her alcoholic husband and his secret. We both ended up seeking solace in each other and one night, when Frank had passed out in an alcoholic stupor, Myra came to my home and cried on my shoulders. You can probably guess the rest. I was grieving over the loss of my mother and Myra had caved in under the strain of her life with Frank.'

Joel's face changed to tomato red and Hope wasn't sure where to look.

'How did Frank take that? Did Mum tell him?'

'Yes, she did. He knew he hadn't been a proper husband to her and agreed to support her by raising you as his own daughter. It would have caused such a scandal in the fifties if anyone discovered the truth. All three of us had to keep a pact that no one else would ever know. Frank also had his own skeletons in the closet and that remained a secret too.'

'I can't believe that I've found the truth after so many years. I had my suspicions and gut feeling that something was terribly wrong all my life,' she spouted.

'Look, Hope. I'm sorry to have to tell you all this. It's not pleasant news.' He reached for another biscuit and topped up their coffees.

'Your mother made me promise I wouldn't tell anyone but I can see the impact that all this has had on your life.'

Once again, Hope was fighting back tears of anger. 'Now I know why I never felt loved or accepted by Frank or his relatives.

They aren't even my kin and I guess they all found out at some stage.'

Joel walked over to her and put his arm around her shoulders, while she allowed him to offer her comfort. Then he tried to talk then stammered, his face appearing flushed again.

'I'm so sorry, really I am. Please forgive me, Hope. I've never stopped loving you and it was torture for me to be separated from you.'

'Then why did you? Why did you leave without saying goodbye or leave me a note or something? I thought you didn't care about us anymore.'

'I couldn't take it any longer. I wanted your mother to divorce Frank for years but she just felt guilty, always driven by shame, even though she had grounds for the marriage to be annulled. She thought he would not have been able to look after himself if she left, although his drinking was affecting her health. I just couldn't wait for her any longer and gave up hope of ever being married to her. I decided to let her go.'

By this time, Hope couldn't contain herself. She was not only feeling devastated by her own grief but also for Joel, her mother and Frank. Joel and her mother had let her down by leading her to believe a lie all these years.

'Look, Hope. At some point, you'll have to forgive your mother, just as God has forgiven you. If you keep holding onto all that resentment, it'll make you sick.'

Hope was taken aback. Until now, she'd not heard any God talk coming from Joel. In fact, she could never remember him attending any kind of church.

'What do you mean? Why are you bringing God into all of this?'

'I've been converted. I have close Christian friends who live locally and who kind of rescued me when I met them at the Horse Breeders Association. They saw the bad state I was in when I purchased this ranch and invited me to their home for meals and then to their church.'

Hope didn't know what to say as she was both in disbelief and ecstatic that her own father had become a Christian. She wanted to cry out— Dad, you've found faith too, just like Jessie and her family. But instead, she changed the subject.

'Look ... I don't hate Mum. I just feel angry that she betrayed me all these years. I'm not ready to forgive her, not yet.'

'I'll have to work on that now, won't I?' Joel was trying to help Hope loosen up as he could see the strain on her face with the significant disclosures he had made.

'Dad— can I call you that?'

'Of course, my love, you must call me Dad, as I am your father. Look ... we could both get a blood test that can prove it. How about it?'

'Sure. It's not that I don't believe you, but it would make it more real if I could see it in writing. This means that Nelly is my Auntie. You need to talk to her Dad. Tell her the truth too.'

'She already knows, my love. She also kept silent all these years. She'll be relieved to know it's all out in the open now. I'll phone her and we could visit her together sometime.'

'It's pity she hasn't got any children. I would have cousins.'

'But we all have each other. God is gracious.'

'Let's wind it up with a little prayer, shall we? Will you let me pray for us all, Hope? Is that okay?'

She nodded her head in agreement and as she closed her eyes, Joel took her hand in his.

An enormous weight lifted from her shoulders. It was like old times with Jessie when she used to pray for her and hold her hand. For the first time in years, she felt secure and loved.

Chapter Eleven

Eighteen months later at Dart River Ranch

Joel had become involved in the wild horse advisory groups and the horse welfare organisations in the south after he arrived in Paradise.

He had taken upon himself the responsibility to rescue the wild horses in the hills around Glenorchy from poachers and blood-thirsty pleasure seekers who try to shoot them. The herd included many Kaimanawa horses that the renowned ex-army officer Captain Carl Richardson from Australia had purchased from the army and transported to his expansive ranch in the Dart Valley several years prior to Joel's arrival.

There the Captain suffered a devastating blow. As his men were unloading the horses, they failed to secure the pen adequately and his two prized young Arab stallions pushed the fence over and escaped with the Kaimanawa horses. They stampeded and took off into the hills around Diamond Lake where tourists have seen them appear on occasions, grazing peacefully by the lakeside. The herd has doubled in size.

Due to the loss of the stock and other unfortunate financial setbacks, the Captain had been declared bankrupt and his ranch had become a mortgagee sale. No one in the valley heard from him again. Hunters have tried shooting at the horses each year during the hunting season as they often frighten off the deer. Joel had been given the name "horse whisperer" by the locals and his team of musterers who assisted him each year.

***

Hope became adept at handling Misty on the steep slopes around Dart Valley and was deemed capable enough by her father to be able to take part in the next big muster.

Her university studies by correspondence took up most of her time. This year she'd spent two semesters living in student quarters attending the university full-time and graduated with a Diploma in Equine Health. Even though she'd been to visit her mother in Bethlehem a few times, she only went to keep the peace.

She couldn't wait to get back to her home which was now Dart River Ranch and looked forward to riding Misty.

***

At last, no more study. Hope was ecstatic as her old Toyota chugged its way down the long drive towards Dart River Ranch. Joel stood on the front porch as always, waving as she approached the homestead, which was the thing that she looked forward to most. Seeing her father standing there greeting her with his broad smile. It was still spring with snow in the foothills which meant Joel had the wood fire burning. She could tell, as there was a strong smell of tea tree lingering in the air.

Cole had finished his university degree and had been working full-time for Joel helping him with the breeding program and training young horses.

He peered surreptitiously through his cottage curtains every few minutes, craning his neck to see if the Toyota was parked in Joel's driveway. At last, he heard the familiar sound of Hope's vehicle arriving and pulling to a halt. He quickly ducked behind the curtains, as he did not want Hope to see that he was more than eager to see her. It'd been six months since he saw her last and he wondered how much she'd changed.

Joel walked down the steps, gave Hope a hug, and took her bags as she followed him inside. Then Cole noticed Joel walking back outside again and waved out to him, hoping to catch his attention, which wasn't really necessary. Joel had told him early that morning that he would let him know when Hope arrives so that he could drop over to partake in a welcome-home meal.

Cole ran back into the bathroom and had a last minute check of his grooming. He was clean-shaven, but today his hair played up. He had thick brown hair that he tied with a band into a small ponytail. It made him look far from effeminate as it outlined his fine contoured jaw and square face. He picked up his brown leather Stetson and raced out the door but as he neared the house, he pulled back and sauntered slowly up the steps onto the porch.

'Are you there Joel? Can I come in?' Cole walked in without knocking.

'Only if you're good looking.' Joel winked at Hope and colour rushed to her cheeks.

'We're in here.' Joel called from the lounge where he'd just stoked the fire.

'Oh—Howdy, Hope!' Cole spoke as though he'd no knowledge of her arrival but his pretence was unconvincing to Hope.

'Hi, Cole. It's been such a while since I've seen you and you look different.'

'Yep, I suppose I do. My hair's grown long and I expect my face is more leathered.' He combed his fringe back quickly with his fingers.

Hope did not let on that the leathered look appealed to her. So did his warm brown eyes. She'd not been interested in males at university. She'd thrown herself into her studies and it left no time for socialising. And even then, she'd no previous hankering to get into a relationship. She enjoyed being a free spirit and her horse was the only love of her life. But this time, something unusual awakened in her when Cole walked through the door. They'd only ever had a platonic relationship and that's how Hope had intended it to stay.

'Right, you two. Why don't you have a good catch up while I check the roast in the oven?'

'I'll give you a hand.' Hope stood up and followed Joel into the kitchen.

'No, honestly, I don't need any help. I'd rather Cole brought you up to date with what's happening at the ranch and our plans for the big muster.

Hope and Cole sat awkwardly as though they'd just met and chatted away about the ranch, then Cole changed the subject.

'Your father told me your twenty-first birthday is coming in a few months.'

'Yeah, I forgot about that. Dad said he wants to organise a birthday party for me but I don't know many people around here. Just our staff and a few friends from church who live locally.'

'I can't believe it's been almost two years since you first arrived at Paradise. It'll probably be good for you to get to know some of

the locals socially. I think you should give your father the
opportunity to do something for you.'

Hope sat there wondering how much Cole knew of her past,
but unbeknown to her, Joel had already told Cole he was Hope's
father.

'I hope you're ready for the big muster. There are some fine
looking breeds up in the hills. A few new ones we haven't come
across before.' Cole's hat was still on his head and he hadn't
noticed until Joel nodded at him, trying to indicate he needed to
remove it. He placed the Stetson next to him on the couch.

'I can't wait. I've been so looking forward to this. What will you
do with them all? You won't be able to keep them all on the
ranch, surely.' Hope looked at him, eyes wide.

'I don't think there are many left. Perhaps just one or two
herds, about twenty horses, I suppose. We'll break them in and
sell them, or other trainers will buy them and break them in
themselves. We'll use some of them for breeding. Joel has
received orders from further up the island from trainers who
want new stock.'

Joel poked his head around the door. 'Come on you two. Let's
tuck in. Hope, would you mind setting the table? Cole, why don't
you pour us some of that Speights ginger beer? It's a good brew
that one.'

For the first time since Hope left Jessie's home, she felt like
she had a family. Cole had become like a brother to her and her
father doted on her as she did him. But this time, she noticed
there was a change in her father.

'I think it would be a good idea if we give thanks to the Lord
for our food and all our blessings. If you don't mind, both of you,
I'll give thanks before we eat.'

Hope's life was about to take an unexpected turn. A cold southerly wind pierced the rugged mountain foothills where the small team of musterers headed. The alpine climate cooled everything down rapidly and Hope felt the chill penetrate her lungs in spite of the thick merino garments she wore under her oilskin jacket.

'Now, Hope. You'd better ride with me and remember the instructions I gave you about not getting in their way. If the herd stampedes, you move quickly and follow me.'

Joel pulled his horse up alongside Misty and waited while Cole acted as a scout, moving up behind the ridge to see how far away the herd was. He moved quietly and slowly with the dogs creeping silently beside him.

Hope shook with an adrenaline rush. This was her first big muster, a full herd. *I hope I don't muck it up.* 'Shhh, Misty, go quietly now,' she whispered as Misty shook her head a few times then stood still as a post.

'Just stay with me Hope and don't do anything unless I ask you. Things can turn to custard pretty quickly.'

As Hope searched his face, she could see regret that he'd brought her with them. It unnerved her slightly. But she'd persisted until he gave in.

She felt the strong freshening wind bite her cheeks as she snapped the domes to fasten her jacket collar. The waiting on the ridge for Cole to return felt like forever. Suddenly, like a tornado rushing at them, the horses came towards them, stampeding through the trees.

'Quickly! Follow me!' Joel rushed off towards a group of trees.

Hope could see the wild horses galloping towards them through the forest clearing with Cole trying to restrain his horse along the fence-line.

'What's going on?' Hope caught up to Joel looking over her shoulder at Cole further back on the ridge, whose horse was almost out of control. The herd rushed past him.

'Something spooked them. This doesn't usually happen. Hey! Quiet!' Joel growled at one of the dogs that started whining.

'They'll get away on us now. They are far too charged up to muster like this. I'll find out from Cole what happened when he gets down from the ridge.'

Without warning, a tall, black stallion turned around and veered towards them bearing its teeth and flashing the whites of its eyes at them.

'Quickly, get in there behind the trees while I deal with this!' He pulled out a stock-whip to protect himself.

Hope dug her heels into Misty, adrenaline racing through her veins. She charged down the ridge behind a thicket of young pines and as she reeled around, Misty lost her footing and went down onto her knees trying to stay upright then struggled back up. Hope flew off and lay sprawled on the grass. Misty had tried not to squash her but had caught her head with a hoof. The culprit stallion let out a mighty grunt and disappeared in a cloud of dust.

Joel was horrified. He dismounted in panic, dropping his reins while his trustworthy steed stood and waited. He slid down the tussock grass to find his precious daughter bleeding and unconscious. Misty stood nearby, back on her feet and limping a little.

'Hope, Hope! Wake up, please!' He felt her throat for a pulse and checked her breathing. She appeared lifeless but breathing. Her pulse raced. Then he saw blood on his hands. When he inspected her head, there was a deep gash at the back of her scalp that bled profusely. By this time Cole had arrived on his horse overlooking the ridge looking down at them.

'What's happened? What's wrong with Hope? Can I help?' He yelled, oblivious to the incident.

'Go to the nearest homestead and call the doctor. Tell him she'll need to be airlifted to the hospital and to come quickly. She's unconscious. Bring a blanket back too. She's in shock and it's freezing up here.'

'So sorry, Joel. My horse got spooked just as I approached the herd from behind. A young Buck appeared from behind a bush. My horse reared and I hit my head on an overhead branch and yelled. It must have skittled them.'

'What the ... the deer aren't usually this far down. It's okay, Cole. I understand ... but please go as fast as you can. You'll have to let the workers in the stockyards know. They're still waiting for us below to bring the herd down. Tell them they can go home until further notice.' Cole moved away, carefully winding his way back down the valley.

Joel took off his thick, oilskin vest he wore over his fleecy swanndri and draped it over Hope's chest. Misty just stood nearby, head hung low as though she knew Hope was hurt. Joel thought she was going to die. She appeared inanimate as he stared at her deathly translucent cheeks. He kept touching her neck to check her pulse. He wiped his tears away with the cuff of his Swanndri and cupped his face in his hands.

'God, why? I've only just got her back again. Don't let me lose her now!' He collapsed onto the cold ground, pounding the earth with his clenched fist.

'I beg you. Please save her! I know I shouldn't have let her talk me into bringing her here. It was my guilt I suppose for having let her down all these years. Now I've made it worse. Please let her be alright.'

Chapter Twelve

Cole brought back the blanket and another jacket for Joel. 'The local doctor can't come as he's attending a birth. He's organised the rescue helicopter and said to turn her onto her side and keep her warm.'

'Thanks—I've already rolled her over. Here … give me the blanket.' He wrapped the blanket around her and used a corner of it to place under her head on top of the blood-stained grass.

Another thirty minutes of waiting seemed like hours. It was torturous for Joel who kept checking her breathing and pulse obsessively. Suddenly he heard the deafening drone of the helicopter's rotors above and almost cried with relief.

Two doctors and a nurse had to land further down the valley where it was flat. They strenuously clambered up the incline to where the patient lay, dragging the stretcher and medical gear with them. Hurriedly the doctors assessed her vital signs.

'We have to move quickly! She's in shock and her blood pressure is very low.' One of the doctors quickly introduced himself as an Intensive Care Registrar. 'Dave's my name and this is John, another Registrar. Quickly— John, get that intravenous line in. We need to get her blood pressure back up. She has a bad gash in the scalp here and will need stapling when we get to the hospital. I'll apply a pressure dressing for now. We need to get her out of here before she deteriorates.' Dave appeared agitated and kept taking her pulse.

They laid her on the stretcher and asked Joel if he wanted to accompany them in the chopper.

'You might like to come along in case she regains consciousness on the way. You can stay at the hospital until you decide what to do.'

'Yes—yes, of course. I ... sure, I'll come.' He turned to Cole who appeared like a dog that had been scolded, even though he wasn't to blame.

'Cole, I'm sorry, mate. You're going to have to walk Misty and my horse back to the ranch and get the vet to check Misty. Are any of the boys still down below?'

'Yep. Two of them are still waiting down there in case you need them.'

'They can take our horses back. Tell them I'll sort their hours out later. You can go back to keep an eye on the ranch. But don't forget to phone the vet.'

'I already radioed them— they know what's happened. They're waiting for instructions.' Cole gathered up the reins of the other two horses and led them away.

'Come on— you need to get into the chopper.' The doctor directed Joel safely onto the aircraft after Hope had been fastened into the receiver for the stretcher. The nurse covered her with more blankets and fiddled with the intravenous tubing.

Joel started blowing on his hands and rubbing them together as if he was feeling the cold.

'Please strap yourself in sir. Here is a blanket for you also.' The middle-aged nurse in black trousers and a thick jacket with fluorescent stripes put her hand into a deep pocket and pulled out a small bar of chocolate.

'You might need this to help you with shock. It must be difficult for you.' She handed him a small bottle of electrolyte drink then turned her attention back to Hope.

'Thanks, the wind was biting up on the ridge. Please tell me ... what are her chances? How bad is her head injury?'

'It's not really for me to say. The doctors will talk to you when we arrive at emergency care. They'll take her straight to the intensive care unit.'

'I mean ... all the bleeding. Will she be brain damaged?' He took a few gulps of the beverage, suddenly realising how dehydrated he was.

'We can't assess her properly until we stabilise her. We'll know more then. But the gash on the head did not pierce the skull. It's just a deep scalp wound. She'll need a skull x-ray.'

Joel relaxed his jaw as he listened intently. He focused on the nurse with a fixed gaze as she took Hope's blood pressure and shone a small pupil torch into her eyes.

'Still nothing?' Joel went to undo his seat belt as if to approach Hope.

'Ah ... please stay buckled ... It may just be a temporary situation. She could become conscious at any time. You'll find out more once we're at the hospital.'

Joel slumped back into the seat, as though finally accepting his powerlessness over the situation. He softly prayed again. 'Help her ... please Lord. She's not had a happy life and I want to do things right this time. Please give me the chance.'

The nurse looked back at him and he looked away, averting her gaze. *I hope she didn't hear me ... I thought I was just praying quietly.*

'Are you okay over there? We should be landing in about ten minutes.' She gave him a sympathetic smile. Even her eyes smiled.

***

Joel was instructed to wait in the room outside the Intensive Care Unit where Hope lay attached to numerous pipes and tubes, though not artificially ventilated.

'Can I bring you a cup of tea or coffee, sir?' A hospital assistant stood in the doorway with a trolley.

'Tea with milk would be nice, thank you.'

'I've been told to offer you a hot dinner. We usually do when relatives arrive for the first time.'

'That would be great. I haven't eaten all day. Just a small one if you don't mind.'

He suddenly saw Hope's doctor leaving the Intensive Care about to walk down the corridor.

'Excuse me— Dave. Sorry, but I need to know what's happening with my daughter.'

'Oh, yes ... I was going to come and talk to you. I'm just going to look at her skull x-rays and I'll be right back.'

Joe thanked him. He slid down into his armchair and wondered what he was going to do if this went on for days. He'll have to phone Cole and ask him to keep the ranch going with back up. What about Myra? She'll have to be informed.

He looked around to see if there was a phone. The hospital assistant came towards him again pushing the trolley.

'I've come to get your dishes. I hope the hospital food was palatable.' She roughly dumped the dishes on top of the over-stacked pile.

'Thanks, the chicken was good. I was wondering if I can make a couple of long distance calls to let Hope's other family members know what has happened.'

'Of course. Close family can make long distance calls as long as you keep them short. Just go to the front desk at Reception and ask them to put the call through to the private room. I'll show you where that is.' She gestured to him to follow her down the corridor and muttered something to the receptionist.

'Of course. Mr Grey— just write the number down and I'll put the call through to the private family room.'

'I have two calls to make if that's okay.'

'No problem. There's a limit of six minutes per call. When you finish the first call, hang up, and then dial zero. I'll answer and put your next call through.'

Joel thanked her and walked off, shaking his head. How antiquated the system was. It would be easier to just phone with a coin box.

Myra answered the first time. 'Joel, is that you? How is Hope? I haven't heard from her for a while.'

'That's why I'm ringing, Myra. There ... there's been an accident,' he stammered. 'She's taken a tumble off Misty when the horse went down.' He was fighting off the guilt and held his breath, waiting for Myra's reaction.

Her response was predictable. Joel's voice shook and he struggled to swallow as though he was choking. He longed to be there to comfort her as she said that Doug was out for the day.

Now she was receiving the impact of this news alone and he waited for her to compose herself. His voice softened even more. 'I'll pay for your flight to Dunedin. I can book you into a motel near the hospital but I'm not sure where I'll stay yet. The hospital told me I could spend a few nights on the ward.'

'I have my old friend Elma who lives close by. I'll give her a call.' She burst into tears again.

'Listen —I have an idea. I need to stay here too, so I'll get Cole and one of my ranch hands to bring my Ute up here. I can pick you up from the airport and take you to your friend. Then I can book a room for myself at the motel next to the hospital and come and get you each day.'

Myra calmed down. Now she wasn't alone in all this and Joel needed her support too. While he was winding up the conversation, Hope's doctor poked his head through the door.

'Sorry to interrupt,' he said quietly. I have some results for you.'

Joel waved his hand at him to let him know he had finished his phone call.

'Myra, I've got to go ... the doctor's here. I'll call you back later tonight once they've given me a report. I have to call Cole now too.'

***

The two ICU doctors in their blue medical scrubs were hardly distinguishable from the rest of the staff. But they were the doctors who had brought Hope to the hospital. Joel felt relaxed with them as they sat around the table, showing him the x-ray reports.

'Well, we have some good news. Hope does not have a skull fracture. She definitely has had a hard knock and is still unconscious but there have been eye movements. This means she is drifting in and out of consciousness. It's a waiting game, I'm afraid.' Dave appeared to set his jaw, frowning as though he was concerned.

'What does that mean? Will she come out of the coma?'

'There's a good chance she will. Her vital signs are returning and the fact that she's been breathing on her own all this time means she has only sustained a mild traumatic brain injury which we call TBI.'

'Can I go and see her? Will she be able to hear me?'

'You can sit with her but not say anything to disturb her. Just reassure her that you are there and let her hear your voice. Tell her that her horse is safe. She may become disturbed about that if her memory starts to return.'

David accompanied him into Hope's room. Her face was not so pale and she was breathing normally. David left the room and Joel pulled the chair close to her bed and took her hand. It was much warmer now. Unlike the hand he had held on the ridge in Dart Valley which was like the hand of a corpse, ice cold and motionless.

He kissed her cheek and spoke softly in her ear. 'It's Dad, Hope. I'm here— you're going to be okay. You've had a bad fall but you're in hospital in good hands. I love you my precious and I'll wait here until you wake up.'

He was sure he felt her hand move in his. Perhaps he was just imagining it. He was overcome with fatigue and lay his head on her bed next to her.

He must have drifted off to sleep and awakened with a start. His mouth was dry and he asked a nurse for a glass of water.

'There's a water fountain along the corridor. I'll get you one. I'll be in to take your daughter's recordings soon.'

The nurse with the kind face gave him a paper cup of water and he thanked her and resumed his night watch at Hope's side.

Later on, when he checked his watch he saw that he must have been asleep for an hour. He took Hopes hand again and chatted away to her as he watched her eyelids flicker. Now and then they would stay open and as he tried to make eye contact with her, he was aware she was in another world.

He started to tell her how well Misty had been doing.

'You wouldn't believe it, Hope. One of our new stallions in the paddock next to Misty has been trying to get friendly with her. Of course, I kept them apart but he's pretty keen. She missed you while you were at university so you had better wake up so I can take you home to her.'

He made sure he didn't tell her that Misty was limping and had hurt her shoulder when she fell. Nothing serious but will take some months to heal.

Joel could hear the nurse doing her rounds, dragging a small trolley along the corridor with her recording equipment.

Just before she arrived at Hope's door, Joel nearly jumped through the roof with excitement. Hope squeezed his hand. *Am I imagining it?* 'Hope, darling … it's Dad— I'm here! Please open your eyes.' He felt her squeeze his hand again. 'Oh, my love, you're going to be okay.' Tears stung his eyes.

'Did I hear you say she's waking up?' The nurse stood at the door and Joel wasn't sure how much of his conversation with Hope she'd heard. He quietly resented her interrupting his special moment with Hope as she slowly gained consciousness.

'She's been squeezing my hand. I'm sure it was in response to my voice.'

'That's wonderful. I'll let her doctor know. I've some medication to put into her drip infusion. It'll calm her down as she wakes from her coma and it'll keep her from becoming agitated.'

'How long do you think it'll be before she completely wakes up?'

'I can't tell you that. None of us can. But she's showing positive signs of having sustained a mild brain injury. I'll continue to monitor her half hourly during the night.'

Joel looked at his watch and calculated that Hope had been unconscious for twelve hours since her fall at ten that morning. His eyes burned as he fought the fatigue but pushed on, determined to be at her side when she gained consciousness.

At midnight, as he started to drift off to sleep with his head on her bed, Hope tugged on his hand and opened her eyes then muttered something incoherently. She startled him. A jolt shot through him sending a shiver down his spine. He reached for the bedside medical call button and her nurse came running.

'She's waking up ... she said something and opened her eyes.' Joel stood over Hope and tried to get her attention but her eyes stayed fixed on something to the left of him, then to the right. She wasn't able to make eye contact with him. She just lay there staring into space.

'What's happening ... why is she doing that?' He tried hard not to panic.'

'It's normal when someone is gaining consciousness. Don't worry. Just give her time.'

Her doctor arrived quickly and began to assess her. Minutes later he turned to Joel with a jubilant look on his face. 'Well, Joel, I think she's going to pull through. She's a fortunate young lady, that's all I can say. Just keep talking to her calmly and reassure her as you've been doing. I'll be back in an hour.'

Both the nurse and doctor left the room. Joel broke down crying with relief. He tried hard to suppress the heavy sobs then blew his nose and sat down in the chair next to Hope's bed thanking God. His maker had come through for him again.

As he prayed, he heard Hope utter the word Dad, then she said Misty's name. At that sound, Joel knew she would soon be home.

<h1 style="text-align:center">Chapter Thirteen</h1>

Joel collected Myra from the airport and they stayed near the hospital for the next three weeks visiting Hope each day. They had a lot of catching up to do and this was a good time to do it. Especially with so much time to fill in outside visiting times. Cole had faithfully dropped off Joel's Ute and gone back to the ranch with his colleague.

He pulled up outside Elma's gate. Myra climbed into the passenger seat. Before Joel drove off, she touched his hand. 'Elma says you can sleep in her sunporch to save you money. As long as you chip in for food and power. She's on a pension and is not well off.'

'Are you sure? That's kind of her.'

'Well, staying in the motel for nearly a month will cost you a fortune.'

'You're right about that. I've been there a week already and they know how to charge. It was the only motel next to the hospital. I'll get my belongings this evening and come over. Let's get back up to the Neurology ward. Her doctor wants to talk to us today.'

Hope had been out of her coma for over a week, but she was muddled and suffered from amnesia. Her doctor directed Joel and Myra into his consulting room.

'There have been some promising signs of recovery taking place but the road to healing can be wrought with twists and turns.' He pushed both hands into the deep pockets of his white consulting coat and sat back on his chair.

'Hope has been having bad flashbacks, yelling out as if she's arguing with someone.'

'What kind of things has she been saying?' Myra pulled nervously at her fingers and glanced at Joel.

'She keeps calling the name Misty. "You can't take Misty from me", and starts crying. Then she acts as though she's lost and looking for her father. She often cries, "No, Mum, you can't stop me!" Do you have any idea what it could all mean?'

Joel's eyes filled with tears and Myra's face showed a tormented expression.

'She appears very troubled. Has she suffered a traumatic emotional event prior to her fall?'

Myra tugged on Joel's arm. 'Please, can you tell him ... I mean about Misty and you and I.'

Joel gave his nervous cough and sniffed loudly. He spoke with a husky voice and told David the long story. Before he finished talking, Myra had crossed her legs and folded her arms tight, appearing defensive.

'Look, Mrs Petersen. I understand how difficult it has been for you, but while you're visiting Hope, it's advisable not to enter into any dialogue with her until she is in complete recovery. This issue over her horse going missing like that has caused some deep-seated resentment. Her conflict with you is now manifesting itself again. We don't want her to regress at this point in her recovery.'

Myra stammered. 'Are you trying to say I shouldn't visit her? I came all this way to see her.'

'Oh, no, of course not. I just meant that we need to stop her from getting agitated in any way while her brain is on the mend. Just sit quietly with her and let her say something if she wants. She has to stay calm at all times until she is stabilised.'

Myra slumped further into her chair looking even more despondent. Joel leaned over and stroked her arm.

'We can handle this, don't worry, Myra. We'll work this out together.'

Doctor Dave, as Joel called him, left and they both went to sit at Hope's bedside. She lay quite still then became vocal, jabbering away incoherently. Occasionally she recognised Joel or Myra and spoke a few lucid words to them. Myra just sat smiling at her and holding her hand while Joel placed his arm around Myra's shoulders and held her tight. It was a healing journey not only for Hope but also for Myra and Joel.

***

A month after her accident, Hope was discharged from hospital and could travel back home. She was getting along much better with her mother than ever before and Myra did not want to part with her daughter. She was reluctant to return to her own home and had not yet booked her flight. The day of Hope's discharge, Joel took Myra for lunch at a little café across from the hospital, to say farewell.

He reached across the table and took her hand. 'Look, Myra—Hope has been very happy at the ranch and has been working on forgiving you. We've been attending a little church there and my life has changed too.'

Myra gazed at him and her mouth dropped open.

He continued. 'Why don't you come back with her? You can sit next to her in the Ute. It's very comfortable at the back. Why don't you stay for a week and see how you like it. There's nothing for you in Bethlehem now that Frank's gone and Doug is independent and working at the hospital.'

'What do you mean? Come to live in Paradise?'

'Yes. We could all have a fresh start. You know I've always wanted to marry you but I couldn't sit back and watch your life disintegrate with a drunken dependant any longer. I saw your soul being eaten up inside and your life disappearing before my eyes.'

'I ... I don't know, Joel. I'll have to sell the house and what about poor Doug? Where will he live?'

'Why sell the house? I have a large home on the ranch with plenty of room. Doug can stay in the house and get someone in to share it with him if he needs company.'

'I don't think he'll miss my company. He's never home and I think he has a sweetheart at work or somewhere he is not telling me about.'

'Myra – why don't you marry me. Please, will you marry me? We've been friends for a long time and I thought I would never see you again. God works in mysterious ways and he has used this dreadful accident of Hope's to bring us back together, his way.'

'I suppose you're right. It sounds a sensible thing to do.' She fumbled nervously with her table napkin.

'But do you love me, Myra. Are you still in love with me just as you used to be? I don't want you to do it just because it's sensible!'

Myra could see he needed the reassurance of her love for him and leaned over, kissing him on the lips in public, regardless of the customers watching at the table opposite.

'Yes—yes, of course, I'll marry you. I can't believe this is happening to me. It's a dream come true for me too.' Her eyes began to mist over. The crevasses in her forehead disappeared.

He took her hand, stroking it as they sat and discussed how and when they would break the news to Hope.

'We'll have to wait until she's well out of the woods. We don't want to set her back now she's in a good recovery. I'll just tell her you're coming to stay with us to help take care of her.'

'Don't worry about a ring, Joel. That will make it obvious. There's something I need to say to you. Please listen to what I have to say.'

Joel could see from the way she was twisting her hands and pulling at her fingers that she was struggling to discuss a sensitive subject.

'I'm so sorry my behaviour sent you away. I know you couldn't bear to see Frank wrecking my life. But I had a reputation to keep and we were running a business. For Hope's sake, I couldn't embarrass her by bringing it all out into the open. What would have become of Frank? He was hardly in a state to care for himself and I had an obligation as a wife to stick by him.'

'And he had an obligation to take care of you and his family, which he did not. It's a two-way thing, Myra. A woman in that situation can't be a doormat. You have needs for safety and security too.' He stroked her fingers gently.

'And love. I need love too. Just like everyone else. That's why I've been so bitter and bad-tempered with everyone. Poor Hope. I took a great deal of my anger and resentment out on her. Look what damage has been done.'

'Well, I didn't have to leave like that. It's my fault too. We are both to blame for her troubled disposition. If you come back to the ranch for a week or so, we can slowly make her understand how much we love each other. You could go back home and explain things to Doug once Hope is more settled then return here to start a new life. We could get married soon rather than later. Of course, we'll have to do the decent thing. You'll have to sleep in the spare room as Hope has the guest room. It'll only be for a short time.'

When Joel finished speaking, Myra leaned over the table with her head in her hands and started massaging her temples.

'I hope I haven't put you on the spot, my dear. You don't have to make any hasty decisions. If you need more time to think about what I said, that's your prerogative.'

With that, she sat back up and looked at him, anxiously twisting her wedding ring.

'No, I don't need more time to think about it. I've done nothing but think about all this since I came down here. I'll come for a week or so then go home to get the rest of my things. Doug can stay in the house until he decides what he's going to do.'

'That's what I want to hear.'

Myra's forehead puckered again. 'Hold on— how are you going to support Hope and me with just a paddock of horses? Do you have a viable income down there?'

'Oh, of course, I haven't told you about the ranch yet have I? I'm genuinely well-off now. After I left Bethlehem and sold my house, I put some of the money into shares which I don't normally do. I spent a year working as a casual farm labourer and my shares skyrocketed. Within a year I was blessed with enough to buy my own ranch. The stud farm has been a lucrative business for me and shows great promise. That and my horse breaking. It's my passion now. We were going to run some more riding courses this year but we'll have to see how Hope gets on now.'

'You know I'm rather out of practice dealing with horses Joel, but I'm more open-minded about it now and would love to support you and Hope with this endeavour. I remember our Pony Club days when we first met.'

'I think that we could make a fine team.' His cheeks dimpled as he grinned.

Instead of her usual lacklustre smile, Joel witnessed Myra beaming radiantly for the first time in years.

He stood up abruptly, took her hand, and walked her jubilantly up to the hospital ward to collect Hope.

This was no longer just a pipedream, for now, he had the whole package, after waiting more than twenty years.

Chapter Fourteen

Hope was dressed and waiting for her parents, desperate to go home. The staff said they were sad to see her go seeing she'd been an inpatient for so long. Her eyes brightened when she saw Joel and Myra enter her room.

'Mum! I thought you were going back to Bethlehem. When is your flight?'

'Ah … it's … I cancelled it. Your father asked me to accompany you on the long drive home. He needs me to take care of you until you are back on your feet.'

Hope felt baffled. She was still having a few problems remembering certain things but no longer had amnesia. She sat speechless for a few minutes, sensing a change in the air. Something was happening between her parents. Especially her mother.

'I didn't expect this. I suppose it's okay. Will I have to move out of my room now? We only have the spare room and that's full of junk.'

Joel flinched momentarily as if Hope's remark might offend her mother. 'That's all under control, honey. Your mum is not worried about that. Let's get out of here.'

As they shuffled in a single file past the Reception, the Charge Nurse called out— 'Hold on please, Mr Grey. I have Hope's discharge letter.'

The nurse looked over her shoulder and spoke to one of the receptionists. 'Where is Doctor Armstrong? He needs to sign the discharge letter.'

A voice called from inside the office. 'He's down the ward seeing another patient. I'll get him.'

The doctor trotted hastily towards Hope and her parents, eager to say goodbye and to give a quick summary of his report.

'Hope is incredibly fortunate to have no residual damage after experiencing coma for more than fourteen hours. I tell you, it's nothing short of a miracle.'

Joel looked Hope in the eye. 'It is a miracle, that's for sure. We're really blessed.'

'She may continue to have some post-concussion symptoms such as headaches, fatigue, flash-backs, and memory loss for a month or two, but I'm sure these will eventually subside. Try to avoid stressful situations, Hope and get plenty of rest.' Dave glared at Myra unnecessarily, as the issue between her and Hope had now been resolved.

'What about getting back on Misty? When can I ride again?' Hope interjected.

'Good gracious, Hope. It's a wonder you still want to get back in the saddle. You can get back on Misty in a month, I think. Best to give your brain a good rest first. Make sure you keep wearing your helmet when you're riding.' He looked her straight in the eye.

'I always wear my helmet. I was wearing it when Misty fell,' she spouted. 'Oh, wait on. I think I was wearing my Stetson during the muster. I wanted to be like the others. I mean ... I'm a cowgirl now.'

'No compromise, Hope.' Dave eyeballed her.

'Don't you worry, Doc. She won't be getting back on any horse without a helmet now.' Joel glared at her too.

Myra tucked the discharge letter securely into her handbag as they waved to the hospital staff.

Although Hope was strapped into her seatbelt in the backseat next to her mother, she managed to stretch out her torso and lay her head in her mother's lap. She slept like a baby for most of the long trip back to Paradise. Myra was in heaven— the bridge between her and her beloved daughter that had been broken was now mended.

'Here we are. Alexandra. We've done two and a half hours driving, so time to stretch your legs and stop for food.'

Hope had already just woken up. She looked around, feeling a little disorientated.

'Toilet block over there. Why don't you both pop over while I order our meal.'

'Fish and chips— great. I didn't have that once in the hospital.' Hope came to life all of a sudden.

'It's not exactly health food but I suppose now and then won't matter.' Myra took her arm as they crossed the road to the amenities.

They ate their meal on a picnic table in the sun while it was still daylight. 'Dad ... what's happened to Misty? Tell me the truth. You said she only had a few bruises but she must have really hurt herself when she went down too.'

'Honestly, Hope. She's another miracle. All she has is severely bruised ribs and shoulder. Her left fetlock was injured and swollen. Cole took care of her by cold hosing the leg and keeping her in the stable away from the other horses. But she can walk on it now. The vet said she can be ridden in a month.'

Hope breathed out loudly, a big sigh of relief.

Joel continued— 'She'll be in recovery along with you. I'll ask Cole to walk her around the arena each day as the vet wants her to have gentle exercises.'

For the next two and a half hours of a five-hour journey, they stayed quiet, contemplative, as though grieving and repining over vain regrets. Or was it perhaps joyful expectations?

***

There was no stopping Cole Digby. He wouldn't take no for an answer and practically begged Joel to let him see Hope who was resting on a couch in the lounge.

'Seriously, Cole. Five minutes only and then you can come back tomorrow when she has settled in a bit more.' Joel was even more protective over his daughter than usual.

'Hold on— you haven't met Hope's mother, Myra.' Cole shook her hand and flashed Joel a look of surprise.

'It's okay, Cole, I'll explain everything tomorrow. Myra's going to be staying on for a week to care for Hope.'

Cole walked in with a bunch of wildflowers he'd picked in the field by his cottage. Hope tidied her dressing gown and pushed her hair into place. She took the flowers from him, sniffed them, and placed them on the coffee table. 'They're nice. Thanks, Cole.'

'Looks like I won't be doing anymore mustering.' Hope gave a half smile. 'I didn't know it could go so horribly wrong.'

'It was a freak accident. I've been mustering for years and nothing like this has ever happened.'

134

'Don't beat yourself up ... please don't. They tell me your horse spooked and reared then you hit your head on a branch. That could have been Dad or me.'

'That's true. The wild deer don't usually come over this side of the mountain.' Cole lowered his eyes as Hope studied his face.

'Honestly, I don't blame you for any of this. Please believe me!' She tossed her pony-tail and passed him a chocolate from the box Myra had given her.

'Come and see me tomorrow. I'm going to get bored sitting around here and not able to ride for a month. Oh, by the way ... thanks so much for taking care of Misty.'

Myra popped her head through the door.

"We'll see you tomorrow Cole, perhaps. You can come for lunch if you like.' She walked him to the door, eager to give Hope a rest.

'Thanks. I'm getting a bit sick of my own tucker. I appreciate the offer.'

As Cole wandered off across the paddock, whistling and swinging his Stetson, Myra and Joel let Hope rest while they chatted away about what an impressive young man Cole appeared to be and how happy they were that the two had become such good friends.

Lunch took place in the same way that Hope had experienced when she stayed with Jessie on her folk's farm. Joel started with praying for the food and a prayer of thanks for all God's grace in the way he provides for his family.

Soon after Hope's arrival home from the hospital following her accident, her parents married. It was a quiet, affair because of the nature of their difficult past and they did not want the shame and pain regurgitated by inquisitive tongues. Their pastor came to their ranch and married them on their patio alongside Doug and Hope. Cole and the pastor's wife were witnesses. To Hope, her parents were a perfect match and now she had the family she always wanted. Doug bonded well with Joel, as they'd always been good friends. When they were younger, he often took Doug fishing. Hope and Doug also used to accompany him camping in the Kaimai Ranges.

Now it was goodbye to broken hearts, broken dreams, and broken promises for Hope.

***

Christmas came and went quickly at Dart River Ranch. Hope was still in early recovery and keeping things simple. Doug was on call at the hospital during the whole of Christmas but promised to be down for Hope's twenty-first. Cole shared a Christmas meal with Hope and her parents.

On Boxing Day they all sat out on the patio finishing off the last of the Christmas mince pies while watching the black and white stallions frolicking. They were entertained by them as they chased each other around the paddock bucking and rearing, playfully challenging each other.

***

Hope had been seeing the Neurologist for regular check-ups and the visits were coming to an end.

'Hope Grey, please go to Room Nine!' The voice of the receptionist echoed through the clinic as Joel and Myra followed their daughter down the long corridor to the specialist's room.

'Mr and Mrs Grey isn't it?' The young Neurologist sat them down across from Hope.

136

'This will be your last visit. I think I said I would discharge you this time if there hasn't been any change in your condition since your last follow-up.'

'I'm fine. I haven't had a headache for weeks and my memory is great. I'm back riding, but not show jumping. Just a bit of dressage.'

He nodded at Joel and Myra. 'How do you think she's doing? Is everything back to normal at home?'

Hope sat biting her lip stifling the urge to say that her parents recently got married and that put a smile on her face. Instead, Joel answered, 'Her moods have been quite stable, and as you can hear, her speech is back to normal.'

'And she's been helping Joel around the farm and is a blessing to have at home. We're very fortunate to have her with us.' Myra reached out for Hope's hand and squeezed it.

'I think I can say with assurance that Hope has made a full recovery. I believe you were both right when you told me at the last visit that your church was praying for a healing miracle. I think that's what's happened.'

In spite of Joel trying hard to suppress tears of joy and gratitude, a few droplets ran down the dark stubble on his cheeks. Myra looked up and spotted his reaction and tears filled her eyes too. She cleared her throat.

'Thank you so much for the good report. So ... I guess she won't have to come back for another follow-up?'

Instead of answering Myra directly, the specialist turned to Hope and smiled.

'No— I'm discharging Hope from my clinic today. Unless of course, there's a problem, you have no need to come back again, Hope.'

***

Joel took advantage of the driving time on their way back to Paradise to chat with Hope about Cole and she had nowhere to go to avoid the conversation.

'Your mother and I were wondering how things are going between you and Cole? It's just that you spend an awful lot of time together on the ranch and he seems very keen on you. Has it become serious? Has Cole let you know his intentions with you?'

Hope sat bolt upright all of a sudden in the back seat, watching her father's piercing eyes in the rear view mirror and could see he was serious.

'I hope you don't think we're playing around. What are you worried about, Dad? We're just good friends. I'm not ready for a relationship and I've so much I want to do with my life.'

'Really— are you planning on leaving us and going to some far off land? I hope not.' He gave her a broad smile.

'No, not at all. I want to learn to train and break horses like you and become a partner in your business.'

'Which part is that? The breeding or the horse breaking and training? The breeding program involves most of the hard work.'

'All of it. I was starting to get right into it just before my accident.'

'The reason I'm asking you this is that I think that Cole is completely besotted with you— in fact, I'm sure he's been smitten since that day you arrived at the ranch looking for me.'

'Oh, really? I didn't realise he viewed me in that way. Poor Cole. It's not that I don't like him ... I just haven't thought of him as a boyfriend as he's been more like a brother to me. I have to admit I really missed him when I was in hospital and was happy to see him the day I came home.'

138

'I'm guessing he's picking up your indifference towards him. But don't worry— if you two are meant to be together, it will happen in time, as long as you don't close yourself off from him. Listen to your heart.'

Hope could see her father still watching her body language through his rear vision mirror. He continued.

'I think that you and Cole are very compatible. You have so much in common and you are both skilled riders with similar qualifications. I think we should pray about this, while I'm driving.'

'That's a great idea, Joel. You lead please.' Myra elbowed him. He prayed out loud.

Hope closed her eyes and was instantly reminded of Jessie and her prayers. As her father prayed, her mind drifted off to the times when she desperately grieved not having praying parents and that her parents were not together.

This is a miracle, just one after the other. God has been so faithful and has always come through for me.

***

Max the horse vet patted his hat into place, re-tied his bootlace, and loaded the Ford Falcon Ute with his bags.

'Misty won't need me back here for a while, Hope. You'll be riding her in the next agricultural show I guess. I'll be there with my twins and I'll look out for you. And I agree— I think she'll make a fine broodmare but just wait until she is completely back to her usual self.'

He turned and shook Joel's hand. 'Just give me a call if you think that mare in the back paddock needs some help. Keep her in the stable overnight.'

Max drove off, swerving to miss a deep puddle on his way up the driveway. Joel looped his arm in Hope's and led her back inside the house.

'Mmm, that smells good.' Hope hovered over the fresh scones that Myra placed to cool on the cake rack and picked at one.

'No, not yet. They need to cool down. Oh— go on. Just one. They're a new recipe, dates with lemon, plenty of lemon. What do you think?'

Hope bit off a large chunk. 'Wow! They're awesome. First time I've had a scone with lemon. Nice work, Mum.'

'Hope— I need to talk to you before we have lunch. Something we need to get sorted.' Joel placed his Stetson on a coat hook.

'Sure, Dad. What's up?'

He walked into the living room and slumped into his armchair across from Hope, crossing his legs and clasping his hands on his lap.

'Dad ... don't look so serious. You aren't at a Federated Farmers committee meeting.'

'Sorry, love. I suppose it is a sort of business meeting. I wasn't joking when you first came to live with me that I saw you as a business partner. I think you're old enough. But that's not what I want to discuss with you.'

'Okay, Dad. Get to the point.' She wrinkled her nose as her eyes smiled.

'I know you're keen to have a foal from Misty as she is the right age at seven years old. But you need to understand she'll be pregnant for nearly a year and it would be wise not to wean her foal for at least seven months. It's kinder not to work her during that time.'

Hope squirmed in her seat. 'Oh, I hadn't really thought about all that. I forgot she would be feeding.'

'Just think about it and you need to decide which stallion you want to sire her with. The white Arab stallion is really a grey that turned white, as he got older, like Misty. And Misty is half Arab so you'll get a stronger Arab breed with that one. It may be interesting to use the white Kaimanawa stallion from the herd we mustered two years ago. He has strong Arab features, is a fast animal, and has already produced great show jumpers and dressage horses with local mares. Our clients say the yearlings are calm, easy to control, and ideal for children too.'

Hope stood up and looked out the window where several Kaimanawa stallions grazed. A tall, coal black, noble beast, prominent against the alpine backdrop of snow-capped mountains, stood near a finer built male, a white beauty which caught her eye.

This Anglo Arab's tail protruded like a flag in the air. His thick mane stood on end in the wind as he raced far ahead of the others horses galloping back and forth. His almost translucent white coat glistened in the last of the late afternoon sun rays. To Hope, he appeared not unlike Misty, apart from the freckles on her mare's face. He raced down the hill towards the fence next to the homestead as Hope's eyes stayed fixated on him. He stood still all of a sudden, staring directly at the lounge window as though trying to convey to Hope a message. Could it be a clue as to what her decision should be?

'I think I know the one that will suit Misty. I'll pray about it, Dad, and let you know. I need to think about all the implications of that decision as you described.'

'Come on, you two. Soups getting cold.'

Chapter Fifteen

'Sorry to hear that, Cole. How long do you think you'll be gone?' Joel stood at the door and looked over his shoulder to see where Hope was.

'I'm not sure, but I'll sort something out with my family and let you know.'

Hope, who was busy at the kitchen bench, had overheard the conversation between Joel and Cole. She wandered out to the front porch where Cole was busy removing his boots. 'What's this, are you going somewhere, Cole?'

'Cole's going to have a bit of breakfast with us before he sets off back to Nelson.' Joel nodded at Cole. 'You tell her, please.'

'To Nelson! Why—what's happened?' Hope froze as if she suspected he was leaving for good.'

'It's my brother, Larry. He's had an accident picking apples. The ladder went from under him and he has a badly broken leg. He works with Dad in the orchard in Nelson.'

'Yeah, that's right, I remember you saying you come from Nelson. Is there no one else to help him?'

'Apparently not. There's a shortage of orchard workers where I come from. Dad's lucky to have Larry, especially at his age. He has a Science Degree but doesn't know what to do with it yet.'

'Why don't we talk about it at breakfast? Food's getting cold.' Myra untied her apron and placed the scrambled eggs and bacon in the centre of the table.

'So ... how long will you be away? I suppose until he can walk again?' Hope couldn't let it go. She handed Cole the toast and butter.

'I suppose so. He'll have to stay in plaster for at least six weeks, then who knows how his leg will be after that. I'll get back as soon as possible.'

'Six weeks!' Hope burst forth.

'At least Joel has some casual ranch hands who can fill in while I'm gone.'

'So you won't be here for my birthday. That's a pity.' Hope wilted. She propped the side of her face on her hand, elbow on the table.

While Cole was explaining the situation, she had mixed feelings about him going away. They aren't even in any kind of a relationship. Why was she being so silly?

After breakfast, Joel waved Cole off at the front gate, picked up the mail from the letterbox and went indoors to phone his casual ranch hands. He needed to have cover for the next few months and rang around to arrange extra help.

Hope finished feeding the pregnant mares and mucking out their stables. She wondered how she was going to get on without Cole around to offload her cares on to or to get feedback about her random thoughts and ideas that often invaded her head. She'd always thought of him as a substitute for her brother, Doug.

Joel came off the phone and spotted Hope outside moping around with a disgruntled expression on her face.

'The way she's reacting to Cole's absence— perhaps there's more to this so-called brotherly love than meets the eye,' he uttered to Myra who was standing on the porch. They wandered back inside. Joel went to the wall cabinet and picked up a portrait of Hope hugging Misty.

'Leave her be. She's at that age when she doesn't know what she wants. But I've noticed she's grown out of the horsey girl tomboy stage.'

Myra drew alongside him to look closer at the photo. 'Yeah, I guess you're right,' she said softly.

'She's always been crazy about horses and boys never entered her head. In fact, she once told me she found them boring.' Joel's gaze lingered on the image as if he was reminiscing on days past when he taught Hope how to ride.

'But she's still discovering who she is and it may take a while before she has any kind of a love interest. Anyway— we don't need any more dramas at present, do we?' Myra elbowed him then lovingly put her arm around his waist as they shared a special moment.

***

'Well, Misty— Dad is putting you out with your mates, tomorrow. You're now all healed and ready to run with the other horses. What do you think about having a tiny foal to look after … your own foal? You think about it and let me know. I want to do what's right by you.' Misty nudged her chest, as though she understood then munched away on the carrot she took from Hope's upturned palm.

She spent the rest of the day exercising some of the young horses with her father. It was a tiring day and she still hadn't regained all her usual stamina.

144

'I'm packing up now, Dad and going to have a hot bath.'

'Good idea— I told you about not pushing yourself. Just let your body dictate how much you do. I can manage okay with the boys I've got lined up.'

As Hope walked through the living room, she noticed the newspaper sitting on the coffee table.

She called out to her mother who'd just come inside from feeding the hens.

'Is that this week's local newspaper? I wonder if Dad has seen this article.' The image of the horse on the front page had jumped out at her.

'Yes, it is. Your father brought it back from the mailbox after he waved Cole off. He hasn't read it yet.'

Hope eagerly sat down to read the article.

'Hey, Mum! Come and look at this. It's just what Dad's been waiting for. He's put a lot of work into it.'

'What's that, dear?' Myra looked around for her glasses. 'Wait, here they are— Let me see.'

Hope held the paper up for Myra as she peered over her shoulder. 'At last! God has found a way to stop your father from continuing with mustering those dangerous wild horses.' Myra breathed a sigh of relief as she stood with hands on hips in her apron.

'I'm going out to show him the article.'

Hope rushed out the door to look for Joel, beaming from ear to ear. He was by the stables hosing down the black gelding he'd been exercising.

'Dad— have you read the front page of the paper? There's an article about the Wild Horse Welfare Trust and the Bill has been passed.'

'Let's see!' He lifted his eyebrows, quickly scanning the article. 'We've finally succeeded. All the hard work our Queenstown branch did by campaigning and lobbying has paid off.' Joel turned around and embraced Hope tightly.

'So if we aren't going to bring the horses out of the hills to protect them, how will they stay safe from those monsters who want to make dog food out of them or kill them for sport?' Hope's forehead puckered as she waited for Joel's reaction to her comment.

'They'll be fined heavily or even locked up if they're caught. No one can venture into Dart Valley up onto the hills with a huge horse truck without going unnoticed. The offenders will find that the locals in the area won't let them get away with it either.'

'That's good, Dad. I hate to think the horses will be a sitting target.'

'Anyway, madam— after what happened to you, I'm not in any hurry to muster wild horses again. It's an act of God that he has taken it out of my hands.'

'Where are you going to get new stock from to keep our business going?'

'From our broodmares. It'll just take longer, that's all. I have two stallions hard at work out there.' He grinned then stopped short, aware he may have embarrassed his naïve daughter.

'Look, Hope— I've had some more ideas. How about offering riding lessons for new riders. The closest riding school to Queenstown is more than three hours away.' He walked back into the tack shed with Hope in tow.

'When Cole comes back, he can continue to help with the breeding programme. Your mother is taking care of the foals, and you could manage the riding classes as a small side business.' He went along the row of bridles, checking each one for wear and tear. 'What do you think— are you interested?'

'I don't know … I wanted to get Misty back into the shows and some hunts.'

'Ah, no. Can't you remember what the Neurologist said about that? He said no jumping.'

'No, I honestly can't remember. My memory still lets me down and I have some gaps.'

'Tell you what. You go and get that hot bath you were talking about, and I'll get cleaned up and come inside. I want to talk to your mother and after dinner, we can all discuss our plans for the business and try to put them into some kind of order. Oh, and don't use this blue bridle, it needs re-stitching. I'll send it away next week.' He hung the bridle up on a hook opposite.

'Sure, Dad, I'll have a good soak and then help Mum get the meal.'

Hope loved hot baths. She lay back in the blue cast-iron claw bath she'd filled with bubbles. Myra knocked twice on the door to make sure she wasn't falling asleep, which was a risk while she still had post-concussion syndrome.

She propped her feet up on the end of the bath and stretched her long legs out, fantasising about running a riding school and becoming a partner in her father's business. Poor Misty. She loves the shows and she's too young to give up jumping. But if she goes into foal, she won't be able to do any show jumping or hunting for eighteen months at least. She lay there imagining what a foal from Misty would look like and what a wonderful mother she would be.

'Hope, can you peel the potatoes for me as you promised.' Her mother's voice at the door startled her back to reality. 'Sure,

Mum. Getting out now, I'll be there in a minute.' Hearing Myra's voice was different now. Gone was the bitter, harsh admonishing bellow she grew up with when Myra was married to Frank Peterson. Hope had a whole new life now.

'Fresh mint sauce from your herb garden Mum.' Hope chopped up the mint and tossed it into the jug of vinegar Myra had prepared.

'Absolutely. Roast lamb's not the same without it.'

Joel walked in. He rested his palms on the bench next to Hope. 'I was thinking … we could start planning your twenty-first birthday party. You could invite some of your Pony Club friends and Jessie could come. I can pay for her air tickets to repay her for letting you stay with her all that time.' Hope was aware he was trying to encourage her to socialise more. He had often expressed his concern that the accident had isolated her socially.

Myra quickly jumped in. 'That's a great idea, don't you think, Hope?'

'Sure, sounds okay. I suppose I could make some little cards with photos of me riding Misty and send them out to people I'd like to have at my party.'

'You'd better send one to Cole to make sure he'll return to the ranch by then. I need him here and that might prompt him to get back.' Joel glanced at Hope then quickly diverted his gaze. Her embarrassment was obvious as her neck flushed.

***

Summer was a welcome season for Hope in Paradise. The snow in the foothills had melted but remained on the peaks and the foals and pregnant mares could now be kept outside in the fields instead of inside the stables.

Hope loved to ride Misty up onto the plains and look at the spectacular view of the surrounding mountains. It was like heaven to her, a privileged life for which she gave thanks to God.

As she pulled Misty to a halt to soak up the sun as it began to rise high above the valley, the mare lowered her head to the ground and reached for the new grass. Hope basked in the morning sunbeams that warmed her almost bare shoulders. She suddenly caught a glimpse of Joel waving at her from down below by the front gate. He was gesticulating as if he wanted her to return back to the homestead.

As she trotted up to the gate, Joel leaned his bronzed muscular arms over the high wooden gate and looked at her with a cheesy grin on his face. 'I've some good news for you. The lab test results for Misty are back.'

Hope didn't have to ask what the result was. She could read it in Joel's face.

'She's pregnant ... she is, isn't she?'

Joel nodded and patted Misty's nose, allowing her to lick the salty perspiration on his arm.

'Hallelujah! That's fantastic.' Hope wrapped her arms around Misty's neck.

'The vet said she's about five months pregnant. I suspected she was, although all the fresh grass she was eating just made her appear fat.'

'That's what I thought it was. It's hard to tell by looking at her.'

'Anyway—the vet says she's in excellent health. She'll need a scan now so I'll have to arrange it soon.'

'Wow, things are going to be different around here for you and me now, Misty.' Hope looked the horse directly in the face, as though she understood.

'When Misty's foal arrives, I'll give you the responsibility of it and when it is old enough to be broken in, I'm going to get you to do that. I'll have you well trained up by then.'

'Really? Great! 'Do you hear that, Misty? You and I and your baby will be a team.' She nuzzled her head into Misty's mane.

'Later on, you'll be able to ride that young horse in the shows too. We'll just let Misty have one foal so you can go back to riding her in the shows. No jumping, mind.'

As Joel wandered back towards the barn where he was organising hard feed for a few of the horses, Hope walked Misty slowly back to the paddock that she shared with a few other mares and geldings. Life was about to change for both horse and rider and Hope had come to understand that when one door closes another door always opens. In her case, it had always been for the good of herself and others.

***

There was no word from Cole, except that Joel received a short phone call from him to say he was going to be delayed. His brother's leg would now need surgery.

'What did he say, Dad? Did he say whether he'd be back in time for my party?'

'He didn't mention that. He said he couldn't make any plans until after his brother's operation.'

Joel looked at the despondent look on Hope's face and tried to humour her. 'Have you thought about the proposition I gave you? I think it's right up your alley.'

'You mean about giving riding lessons? Yes, I have and I suppose it'll give me something else to do if I can't be jumping and hunting with Misty. It's something I can offer to the community.'

150

'That's the spirit. Community service is a great thing. Once you start doing it you'll feel a deep sense of satisfaction and reap the rewards.'

'Okay, Dad. But I'm also interested in some income from it as I need to earn a living too.'

'It'll be your own business venture and we can advertise it in the local paper. The rest of the time you can spend with Misty, gently exercising her and when she has her foal you'll be busy with that.'

Joel went out to the kitchen to put the kettle on again. 'Tea anyone? All this talking has made me thirsty.'

'Thanks, love,' said Myra. You can make me one too. Can you grab the biscuits in the tin up on the fridge?'

That night, Hope's head was full of the intrusion of busy thoughts—recollections of the day's events and deep conversations. The soak in the hot bath did not calm her mind as she tried hard to get off to sleep. She was thinking how much she had to be thankful for— such loving redeemed parents and a wonderful life the Lord has given her. Especially healing her after that horrific accident. Then why am I feeling so disturbed? She asks herself.

She tossed and turned most of that night until she heard the rooster crowing. The bright morning sunrays dazzled her as they forced their way through the gaps in her Venetian blinds. She decided to sleep in and try to put the intrusive thoughts out of her mind. It was as if there was still something missing from her life and she couldn't quite put her finger on it. She knew that God should suffice to fill the God-shaped hole in her soul. So why is this happening? She prayed that God would give her the direction she needed. After that, she yielded and a peaceful sleep quickly consumed her.

***

Hope's riding courses in Glenorchy district became well patronised. Most riders who made bookings were mainly university students who came home to Queenstown in the holidays, or local children.

Hope became an astute businesswoman and Joel called her a "real natural".

Myra had always been adept at running the market garden business that she and Frank had owned in Bethlehem until Frank's death. Now she was able to help both Joel and Hope, with book-keeping and running the office.

Hope wondered what Cole would be doing. His ongoing delayed return to Dart River Ranch concerned her. He'd phoned Joel a few times to explain that his brother needed a longer recovery period since his leg had been operated on twice. He'd begged Joel to keep his job open and promised he'd be back. Joel was reluctant to lose him, as he was the best ranch hand and horseman that he'd had working for him. Or is there another reason why Joel wants to hold onto him?

After a busy day running a beginner's class for juniors which was often a challenge for her, Hope stood hanging up some bridles and halters that some of the children had lazily tossed onto a hay bale instead of placing them on the rack where they'd been instructed to hang them.

'Here you are. I've been looking all over for you. This place is so big we almost need walkie-talkies, don't you think?'

'Oh— hi Dad. You gave me a fright creeping up on me like that.'

152

'Sorry, I didn't mean to. I think you'd better come over to the stables. It's Misty … I think she's about to foal. I've already rung the vet.'

Hope abruptly dropped the bridle she'd held in her hand and raced towards the stables. This was the one day she'd been waiting for all year. A special day for her and Misty.

As she entered the stall, her horse gave a soft whinny. Hope quietly approached her and gently stroked her nose. 'It's okay, girl. I'm here now and I'll take care of you. Everything's going to be alright.' Misty rubbed her head on her shoulder and whinnied again.

The vet arrived and declared her fit and well. He suspected it would be a straightforward birth. He spent many hours with Misty while Myra and Hope ran back and forth with cups of coffee and food to keep his energy up.

By early evening, Hope felt exhausted and went for a walk outside under the stars. It was a clear night in early autumn. So quiet one could almost hear a pin drop. As she looked up into the dark abyss at the sparkling diamonds in the sky, she prayed …

'Please God … grant Misty and her foal a safe and healthy delivery and guide the hands of the vet so he can do everything necessary for a good outcome.'

As she turned to wander back to the stall, Joel poked his head around the corner of the shed.

'You'd better come or you'll miss out on a very special moment.'

Hope took off back to the stall and as she walked in, she saw Misty lying on the ground with two legs protruding from under her tale then witnessed the miracle of her pushing out a black, lanky legged, bedraggled filly which brought tears to Hope's eyes.

'She's black ... I thought ...Dad?'

Joel leaned over and talked quietly in her ear. 'Remember what I told you about foals from greys or whites?'

'Oh yes ... they turn white when they get older. Sorry—my bad memory. They're born black or chestnut you said.' Hope continued to stroke Misty's head while the vet continued to help the animal.

While the vet was dealing with the afterbirth, Hope stayed kneeling next to Misty and kissed her on the forehead. 'You did it, girl. You're going to be a great mother. I just know it.'

Joel was quietly standing behind her. 'What are you going to call her?'

'Um ... I haven't even thought about a name. Let me think.' She looked the filly up and down, curling her fringe around her finger.

'I know— just the right name for her. I'm going to call her Marvella. That means a miracle.'

***

Hope spent hours that evening with Misty and the filly, reluctant to leave them and go inside. She heard footsteps across the courtyard. It was Joel.

'Are you still in there, Hope? Your mother's been calling you to come in for your dinner. Come on— don't worry about them. The vet said they're both in perfect health and they'll be waiting for you in the morning.'

'I'm going to take myself off for a long hot bath. I'm exhausted after all the excitement of Misty's new foal.'

Joel walked back to the house with her. He put his arm around her and pulled her close. 'You mean your little Marvella. Your

little miracle. Hmm ... Marvella ... Marvella. I suppose I'll get
used to calling her that someday.' He cajoled.

Chapter Sixteen

Within the two weeks before her twenty-first birthday party, Hope received replies to most of the invitations she'd sent out. But not a word from Cole.

'That's strange, Mum. I thought he would have been one of the first to reply,' she huffed.

Her mother put down the bucket of hard feed cubes she'd been feeding the weaning foals in the stables.

'He'll be hard at work helping his father pick all those apples and apricots he told us about. If he can't come, I'm sure he'll let you know. Am I guessing right that you're a bit smitten with Cole? I thought you'd said he was more like a brother to you.'

'No, Mum, I'm not smitten as you put it. I just need to know if he's coming so we can plan our catering. I expect everyone to at least respond to my invitation.'

Her mother smiled and quickly backed off.

***

The next day Hope got Misty ready to exercise her in the arena. She buckled up the girth and started checking her stirrups when Joel walked up behind her.

'You're up early this morning ... where are you headed now?'

'I thought I should give Misty a bit of exercise.'

'I've something for you to do but you'll have to leave her foal in the stall. Misty can have gentle exercise at this stage, so if you wouldn't mind helping our ranch hand, Mack. He's about to shift the geldings into the back paddock to make room for the mares. They need a good grass feed and the geldings have had a fair go. They could do with slimming down somewhat.'

'Sure, that's okay. Where's his mate, Sam who always works with him?'

'He's off sick, I'm afraid and you might need to help us out until he gets back to work. Your advanced riding courses don't start for another month. Have you got many takers for the classes?'

'Yes, heaps. Thirty people have replied to the adverts already but I'll have to take small groups of about eight at a time.'

'That's great! That's something to look forward to, your own business.'

Hope blossomed when her father encouraged her like that. He'd never lost his kind nature which she loved most about him.

She mounted Misty who stood perfectly still while she adjusted the stirrup straps and then headed over to the stockyards.

Mack was bent over cleaning dried mud out of his chestnut's hooves. As he looked up at Hope, his horse flicked its tail in his eyes. 'Ouch!' He rubbed his reddened eye with the back of his hand.

'You okay?' Hope asked.

'Yep ... will be in a second. I should watch that as it's not the first time.'

'Dad said I'm to help you shift the geldings. I can come back if you're not ready.'

'No— wait. I've finished now. Let's go.'

They utilised the time to catch up as Hope hadn't seen Mack since he'd returned from a shearing contract in Canterbury.

They walked the horses slowly in the heat of the summer's day until Hope beckoned him to stand under the shade of a tall gumtree while she took out her water flask.

'Want a mouthful?' She handed him the flask. He raised his hand. 'No, thanks. I've got a bottle in my saddle-bag. By the way— I haven't seen Cole for a while. Any idea where he is?'

'Oh, he's gone back home to his folks. His brother broke a leg working in the orchard and now Cole has to fill in to help his father.' Hope tried not to show any emotion.

'Is that right? That's a pity. Except, I don't think that pretty, neighbourly girl minds him being back there. He'll be entertained for a while. Who knows, she might talk him into staying this time.'

Hope felt a large rock drop to her stomach.

'Sorry, I don't know what you're talking about. What girl?'

'His neighbour, Sophie who he always goes on about. They were school friends apparently, and she never leaves him alone when he goes back home. It was quite amusing to hear him talk about her.'

Hope didn't find it amusing. She felt irritated by this conversation.

Well— he's a dark horse. Why did he never mention any of this to me? Maybe that's why I haven't had a reply to my invitation yet.

'How old is this girl Sophie?' Hope said in a disgruntled tone, feeling her neck burn.

'I'm not sure. Cole showed me a photo of her once. Quite a looker she is. Wait— I remember. He went to her twenty-first birthday a couple of years ago. She must be about the same age as Cole. Why the sudden interest in her?' He pulled his horse up as it tugged hard against the bit to grab another mouthful of the rich green grass.

Hope felt a compulsion to interrogate Mack more. But instead, she overcame the temptation and moved Misty on.

'Come on! We'd better get going or Dad will be out looking for us. By the way ... would you like to come to my twenty-first birthday next week? It's on Saturday.' She quickly tried to disguise her disappointment in Cole by inviting Mack, in whom she had no interest at all, to attend her party.

'Sure, sounds like fun. I hope I've got time to shop for a present for you. There's nothing around here so I'll have to get into Queenstown on the weekend sometime.'

'Don't worry, Mack, just bring yourself. Come on, let's get those horses in.' Hope knew it was a knee-jerk reaction she had from hearing Mack's sharing of information about Cole and his neighbourly friend. Is there another side to Cole that she doesn't know about? There has to be a way of finding out. She brooded over this for the rest of the ride.

***

'It's good your party will be over and done with by the time the new riding course starts. We don't want you getting fatigued again like you were after your head injury.' Myra handed Hope the decorations for the grand looking cake she had just finished icing.

'I suppose you're right. It's all been a bit much lately with the new business and trying to get the ranch ready for so many guests. All my Pony Club friends are turning up and Jessie will be

159

arriving tomorrow. She said she'll give me a hand with the coloured fairy lights.'

'Let your father do the fairy lights. We don't want you climbing ladders and risking another fall and Jessie is too short to reach the top of the trees. Just let him do it.' Myra's jaw jutted forward with determination.

Hope's light-hearted mood changed as her mother became overly protective and she tried hard not to snap at her.

'Really, Mum! I'm an adult and I need to live a normal life.'

Hope almost gave in as she saw her mother shrink back as if she accepted her powerlessness.

The nights leading up to her party, sleep did not come easy. Not because of the excitement of her forthcoming twenty-first birthday. But more so because of the intrusive thoughts about her friend, Cole and his friend, Sophie.

Why hadn't he mentioned her name? Hope thought she and Cole had been getting on well and now this.

On nights like these, she jumped out of bed and made herself hot milk with a dollop of honey. That seemed to do the trick.

***

The day before the party, Hope went to the tack shed to check that all the riding gear was in place. She'd planned to take some of her friends riding along the Dart River on her birthday. She took the opportunity this time to rub down the saddles with a leather dressing.

'Where's your elbow grease? You'll have to work a bit harder than that to get a shine up!' Joel stood in the doorway of the shed with a smirk on his face.

'We've had a phone call from Cole. He says he'll be at your party tomorrow but can only stay the weekend. He has to get back to the orchard again as his brother has gone back into plaster after his surgery.'

'Well— it's good he can come but not so good for the ranch that he can't stay, is it, Dad?'

'He said we should rent his cottage out temporarily until he gets back. Mack was looking for another place to live so I'll tell him he can rent the cottage until Cole returns.' Joel lifted the well-oiled saddle back up onto its shelf. He saw the perplexed look on Hope's face.

***

Hope awakened to the sound of the rooster earlier than usual. It annoyed her as she normally slept right through the racket it made at six each morning. She wanted to feel refreshed for her party.

'Jolly rooster! You would have to perch right outside my bedroom. Today of all days.' She opened her window and silently scowled at the rooster, resisting the urge to scream at him.

'Is that you, Hope? You're up early—I thought you said you were going to sleep in this morning to get plenty of rest before the party.'

Myra stood in the doorway holding eggs in the palm of her hand. 'Eggs with your bacon? I want you to have a good breakfast.'

'It was that old rooster. He was so loud this morning. Anyway— bacon and eggs sound great. I'll be there in a minute.' Poor Mother. She just can't come to grips that Hope's a young woman.

Myra kept her talking at the meal table for a reason. Unbeknown to Hope, Joel had been busy in the barn putting up the coloured lights and Mack had arrived with a pile of wooden seats on the back of his Ute.

'Hi, Mack! Thanks mate. Just set them all around the edge of the barn. I can't remember how many she said were coming now, but there are plenty of hay bales for people to sit on. Some guests will stay in the house if they don't want to dance.'

When they'd finished eating, Myra tried to distract Hope from the activities out in the barn.

'Why don't you go and get dressed and then you can help prepare the last of the food. If you don't mind putting all the cutlery and plates out on the trestle tables on the patio. I'll give you a long tablecloth to cover it first.'

'Okay, will do. Jessie's arriving on the two o'clock flight so I'll have to go to the airport around one. She might give us a hand with the food when she arrives.'

When Hope was dressed, she wandered out to the patio and set the table up with a white starched cloth. She carefully placed miniature red roses into delicate glasses. She placed a pile of plates in one corner of the table and the cutlery next to it and wandered over to the fence at the back of the garden. Misty stood there hanging her head over the fence. She threw her head back and whinnied softly.

'Oh, you sweetie. You know it's my birthday, don't you? Wait a minute.'

She quickly went back inside the house to the kitchen. 'Can I have a carrot? Misty has come to wish me a happy birthday. Honest, Mum. She put her head over the fence just now and whinnied at me.'

Hope took the carrot and almost skipped back outside like a child. Misty guzzled the carrot. She licked her hand and gently nudged her chest.

'Thanks, Misty. You're the first one today to wish me happy birthday apart from Mum and Dad.' Aware that her behaviour was very childlike around her animals, she didn't care. It was always a time when she felt like a free spirit, loved and accepted.

***

Jessie couldn't stop talking during the whole trip back from the airport to the ranch. She had noticed that Hope had changed considerably, especially since her accident. She had always been exuberant, full of gusto. Now she was quieter, contemplative, and reserved.

'Well, come on— out with it. Whom are you dating down here? What happened to that spunky rancher who helped you when you had your accident? Remember you wrote to me about him.'

Hope took the deceptive bends in the road cautiously. She had found it hard to focus since her accident. It was the first time she had driven on the windy road to Paradise since long before her injury. She waited until she was on a straight stretch of the road and resumed the conversation.

'He's just a working colleague and friend and he hasn't been here for the last few months. His brother's had an accident and he's had to help run his father's orchard.'

'Oh, dear. So he won't be at your party today? That's a pity. I was so looking forward to checking him out for you.'

'Yes, he'll be here for the weekend.' Hope squirmed and wanted to tell her to stop interrogating her, but restrained herself and quickly changed the subject.

'What about you? Any love liaisons on the horizon?'

Jessie bit her lip and hesitated. 'Good heavens, no. I don't have time to waste on boys at university. I'm doing my finals this year.' She tried to keep a straight face then burst out laughing.

'To tell you the truth, there is somebody. I've had a few dates but we are taking it really slowly.'

They arrived back in time to see Joel and Mack finishing up in the barn.

'You've plenty of time to tell me all about your Romeo while we help Mum finish off the rest of the food preparation. By the way, I forgot to tell you I've changed my name to Grey, my father's name. It's all legal now.'

'I remember in your last letter you were going to sort that out. It's finally come together. God knows you've waited long enough.'

Hope parked the car to the side of the barn as Joel walked over to welcome Jessie.

'It's been a long time, Jessie. You've certainly shot up tall like your father. I have a surprise for Hope. Hop out the front and come and take a look.' Hope grinned at Jessie. 'Wonder what he's up to.'

Joel picked up Jessie's backpack and put it near the front steps of the house then directed them back to the old barn. He opened the large iron door and switched on the fancy lights.

'What do you think, Hope? Your very own barn dance all ready to go.' He turned on the stereo and played a CD with her favourite tunes while Mack broke into a full teeth-baring smile.

'That's amazing! Oh, thanks so much, Dad. You're a darling.' She quickly dried her tears of joy with her sleeve.

'I think it's about time we had a good old shindig around here. As long as all the local cowboys don't wear you out dancing. Life has become far too serious.'

Joel winked at her and she could see he was doing his best to cheer her up after her long, restricted recovery from her head injury. He placed an arm around her neck and gently pulled her back in the direction of the house. 'Your mother is waving at the window— I think she wants a hand with something. Here, Jessie. I'll take your luggage into the guest room.'

'Okay— thank you.' Jessie caught him up.

Mack quickly spoke up, 'We'll see you at the barn dance then, girls,' and walked away chuckling to himself.

At four o'clock, the first few guests had arrived. Joel was outside busy directing them to the car spaces. Some had even walked a good distance and Sam the casual ranch hand had made a few trips in his Ute to collect some of the local young people.

Meanwhile, Hope and Jessie were inside the house fussing over their last-minute face make-up and dress inspections.

'Come on, Hope. Your guests have arrived and you need to be out there to receive them.' Her mother untied her apron strings revealing a trendy black and white polka dot flared dress that contrasted strikingly against her thick auburn hair. She was also in celebration mode.

Hope and Jessie came away from the dresser mirror and bustled awkwardly in their high-heeled shoes to the front door.

Who was the first to arrive but Cole. Hope felt like shrinking, struggling with not knowing whether to feel annoyed or relieved to see him. As she walked onto the front porch, he stopped short, as if mesmerised by seeing this tomboy tough girl in a dress and stockings.

'Well— well! You're a sight for sore eyes.' He winked at her and gave her an alluring smile.

Jessie stayed close behind Hope who sensed her friend was trying to avoid taking away her kudos.

Hope's guests admired her eye-catching elegant attire. Her dress, a light blue floral print flare, with sweetheart neck and pink cap sleeve caught everyone's attention. Her white lace court shoes each boasted a silk flower on the toe.

Hope's neck felt uncomfortably warm and she wanted to hide it while Cole continued to stare at her face.

'Cole! How did you get here? I can't see your car.'

'It's over there by the barn. I've changed it. Dad's bought himself a new one and gave me his Chevy pickup.' He pointed towards the truck.

'No one told me. I like the colour. We certainly wouldn't miss seeing you on the road.

'Yeah. Looks a bit like a fire engine but it's in good nick so I'm happy.'

'It's good you could make it. Come on out to the patio. There's Mum's super punch bowl with a fruit cocktail and there are tables under the trees out of the sun.'

Hope ushered the new arrivals including Cole out to the patio. She placed her gifts on a table her mother had set aside in the lounge. Cole followed her, trying to get her attention.

'I was hoping we could catch up later when you're not busy.' He had hold of her arm, whispering discreetly.

'Mmm ... I suppose so. I'll be busy with the guests handing around the food and drinks. Perhaps I might have time later after dinner before the barn dance.' She cut him short and walked off, leaving him to mingle with the rest of the small group under the oak tree.

Feeling irked, she toyed with the idea of quizzing him about his neighbourly admirer later in the evening. But then again, she could appear fickle, or worse, a jealous fool if she said something. And they're not even dating. Up till now, they'd just been close friends. He has the right to live his own life.

She recalled the song "Fools Rush in" by Ricky Nelson.

Deep down, Hope knew she wasn't ready for any kind of serious relationship and the few young men she had become close to were far too intense, too serious for her. She just wanted to build a long friendship with a young man and see where it leads. Why is it that they just can't regard the affairs of the heart the way she does?

When she finished reprimanding herself for almost weakening, she joined Joel outside. He was still busy finding more parking places for the guests who were arriving one after the other.

'It's okay, birthday girl. You wait up on the porch and greet them at the door.' He waved her back.

Finally, the house and patio were full of babbling guests of varying ages, some of them adult couples, her parent's friends.

The best present Hope was given, was the sight of Doug walking through the door. She hadn't seen him in a very long time and almost felt estranged from him.

He kissed her on the cheek, his thick, wiry beard tickling her face. It was the first time she'd seen him with a beard.

'Ooh— now my face is itchy. That must be uncomfortable in this heat. I don't know how you can stand it.'

'This is a symbol of sophistication, I'll have you know. A distinguished gentleman I've been known as.' He loved playing mind games with Hope.

'You mean extinguished.' She elbowed him then led him down the hall to show him where he'd be sleeping.

'Jessie's in the guest room, sorry, so you'll have to be in the spare room amongst all Mum's knitting and crocheting baskets. The bed's all made up. How did you get here?'

'Mum organised one of your ranch hands to fetch me from the airport … Mack, I think his name is. Very kind of him. Nice fella he is. Told me he is saving hard to buy his own land and start a sheep station. I'm thirsty, where are the beers?'

'Sorry, Doug. It's an alcohol-free party but we've got a large range of alcohol-free cider and wines, even non-alcoholic champagne from an apple orchid in Cromwell, the fruit-bowl of New Zealand.'

'That'll be an experience. I hope I can loosen up enough on that to get you up for a dance, Sis.'

'Mum tells me love is in the air in Bethlehem. Is it true? Who's the lucky woman?' She pulled on his sleeve.

'Mum doesn't waste any time, does she? Just a woman from work I take out now and then. Nothing serious as yet. You just keep the focus on your own love life. I want to hear all about it later.' He wrapped an arm around her waist and walked her back to the lounge. He stretched out in an armchair after he pushed the cat off first.

'Doug—I just want to tell you again how grateful I am that you sent me that money to get down here. In fact, I was able to buy my car, Sunflower, with that.' She bent over the chair and kissed him on the forehead.

'Stop fussing girl and bring me some of that great punch Mum made.'

She brought him a large glass of punch. 'Have some food before it disappears. There are some big hungry farmers around here.'

Meanwhile, Joel turned on the coloured lights that he'd artistically draped around the barn. Earlier in the day, he'd made sure Mack and another ranch hand had shifted the horses to the far paddocks and Hope had also moved Misty.

He checked the microphone and spoke into it.

'Will Hope Grey please bring her guests to the old barn where the music is playing,' then fired up the music.

Hope walked into the kitchen from the patio with a pile of dirty dishes. She heard the announcement again and went back outside to let the guests know the dancing was about to start.

Doug first got his mother up for a waltz, then Hope who was relieved she'd learned to dance at university. While she was enjoying being twirled around by Doug who was a seasoned dancer, Mack had been trying to get her attention, obviously hoping for a dance.

'Isn't that Joel's ranch hand, Mack sitting over there? Perhaps he wants a dance too.'

'Well, he can ask me when we've finished.' Hope was having such a good time with her brother that she egged him on for the next dance, a foxtrot. By the time the music finished playing, the barn had filled with the rest of the guests, and Doug wandered off to talk to Joel.

Hope edged her way along the ornately decorated table with cold drinks, picking up each bottle of alcohol-free wine to read the label. She settled on a pink sparkling wine and as she lifted the glass to her lips, Cole touched her on the shoulder.

'Sorry— what did you say? I can't hear over the music,' Hope sounded terse, waiting for an apology from him for not trying to find her. Let's face it. He'd agreed to have a chat before the dancing started. He could have at least tried to find her. Typical.

'Let's go outside and sit on one of the benches out there under the solar lights.' He gently gripped her bare arm and led her outside. She wiped her forehead, as if to wipe away the tension the conflict had triggered.

Chapter Seventeen

Cole was seated under the pink blossomed cherry tree. Hope walked up to him and plopped herself on the seat beside him reluctantly. She left a calculated gap between them.

He cleared his throat a few times and waited until he had her attention. 'Hope—I don't know how to put this, especially on your birthday. But I feel that since I've been working on my Dad's orchard there's been more than a geographical distance between us.'

Hope tried to swallow a lump in her throat. 'What do you mean?'

'Please don't go all coy on me. You know what I mean. Something's happened between us … I feel you've been giving me the cold shoulder since I arrived.'

'Really? I don't think you've been too concerned about our friendship while you've been away. You appear to have had other things on your mind.' She was struggling to say her piece in an agreeable way and it was noticeable to Cole. *Don't mention Sophie's name … he'll think you're an idiot.*

'Look— there's something I need you to know. Please hear me out.' He cleared his throat again and took a mouthful from the bottle of cider he'd propped up on the old wooden bench.

'You and I have been good mates and work together on the ranch really well. You said to me once that I'm a replacement for Doug and you treat me like a brother.' He hesitated and drank the rest of the cider rapidly as though it was going to give him relief.

'When you had your accident, I remember reaching the ridge on my horse and hearing Joel yelling out to me. As I drew near, I thought you were dead seeing you lying down the bottom deathly still, white as a ghost. Then your father sent me off to get medical assistance and a blanket.'

'I suppose it was quite frightening for you and Dad. Thank you for going to get help. I don't think I ever really said that before.' She kept crossing and uncrossing her feet.

'That's not the point of me telling you this.' He placed his hand on her arm. She flinched then sat rigid, feeling light-headed. She was hyperventilating and knew to slow her breathing down when that occurred.

'Something happened to me that day. I mean—it dawned on me that I couldn't bear the thought of you not waking up and never seeing you again. There hasn't been a day since I've been on my father's orchard that I haven't stopped thinking of you.'

Hope sat bolt upright, her eyes widened as she turned to him with raised eyebrows. She wanted to trust what she was hearing but needed to check out his story and couldn't restrain herself any longer. He heart pounded in her throat. She couldn't hold off another minute.

'I heard from one of the workers that you have someone else back home, in fact, a neighbour you've been seeing.' She felt her blood rush up her neck to her face and was sure her blood pressure had gone up. As soon as she'd spewed out the words, her glare stayed transfixed on Cole's face, determined to see how he reacted.

He laughed heartily. 'Oh, you mean Sophie my next door neighbour. Her family and mine have been friends ever since we were babies. She's like a sister and I find her quite annoying actually. I think she fantasises that our friendship is much more than it is. But honestly, Hope, she's just a neighbour, that's all. I have no interest in her or any other girls for that matter. Just you. I only have eyes for you.'

Hope felt so embarrassed she felt like running a mile.

Now she's done it. He really will give her a wide berth now after her insecure remark.

There was a certain awkwardness between them after Cole's brave act of pouring out his heart to Hope, which she didn't make light of. She just had no idea how to handle his confession.

'Hey, you two! Are you going to stay out there and miss the rest of the party?' Joel had noticed they'd been gone for some time.

'Hope— your mother wants some help with handing around some sausage rolls and you still need to cut your cake before the guests leave.'

'And I'd like the last dance if you wouldn't mind.' Cole ran his hand down the back of Hope's soft black hair and winked. She headed back to the house while he waited in the barn for her. Joel sat down next to Cole to catch up.

'I think Hope's pretty much tickled pink that you were able to make it to her twenty-first. She kept on asking if you'd rung.

You'd better make sure you get her up for that last dance, mate.'
Joel stood back up and walked off with a cheeky grin on his face.

***

That night, when everyone else was in bed, Jessie and Hope lay awake half the night chatting and catching up on all the news.

Jessie got up and sat on Hope's bed. 'So what happened when you two disappeared from the party? You were outside a long time so it must have been pretty serious. I ended up being cornered by your ranch hand, Mack for the rest of the evening … though I didn't mind that at all.' Jessie giggled like a little girl.

'Oh— I needed to check a few things out with Cole. I kind of suspected he might have been involved with a girl back home in Nelson but I was wrong. He seems to be besotted with me.'

'Wow! And what about you? Do you feel the same way?'

'I haven't fallen madly in love if that's what you mean. It's complicated. I really like Cole as a kind of brother or close friend, but I've never had a serious relationship with a man before. I … um…don't know what it is to be in love.'

'Have you prayed about it? What about asking your Dad to pray for you. He's a man of faith now, isn't he?'

'I guess I could ask him. Mum also has God in her life now. Dad led her to the Lord after my accident.'

'That's so amazing! I've been praying for you and your family for so long now. I must tell my folks. And it's a miracle that your mum and dad are together and you are one family now.'

'Yes— thanks to you, Jessie. I really appreciate all your prayers over the years. God's come through for me and my life has changed. It took a huge amount of forgiveness for each one of us. I didn't think I would ever forgive my mother but God's changed my heart. He's transformed us all.'

174

'So, what are you going to do about Cole if he's head over heels about you and you feel differently about him?'

'No, I don't feel differently, I really like him a lot. I think about him often too. Is that love? I just never imagined us having a love relationship and to be honest, the reason is— I'm scared of trusting anyone. I mean ... look what happened with my parents who were so hurt and damaged for years after one bad decision. It makes me afraid to make any life-changing choice.'

'I doubt your parents even considered the consequences of their actions at the time. But this is a different situation for you. Anyway—where's God in all this? You told me that you've put your life in God's hands and trust him for the outcome. That was when you first arrived in Queenstown. So maybe you need to start trusting again.'

Hope didn't like being lectured by her friend and quickly changed the subject.

'What do you want to do tomorrow, Jessie? Cole's only here for two days and asked if I'd go for a ride with him along the river.'

'That's okay. I'm here for a week and your Mum said I can spend some time feeding the foals if I want. I'd love that. You and I have plenty of time to catch up. You go and enjoy your ride with Cole.'

***

The morning after the party, Myra and Joel had been hard at work clearing up much of the mess although the guests had been respectful and well-behaved. Cole joined them all for breakfast as they made their plans for the day.

'Hope— why don't you and Cole go for a long ride along Dart River and into the valley? Misty needs a good run and so does

175

your horse, Pedro,' he said to Cole. 'We've been exercising him for you but only on the ranch.'

'And Jessie is going to help me with the foals in the stables, isn't that right Jessie?' Myra passed her another crumpet. 'I hope you don't mind?'

'Not at all. I can't wait to feed the weaning foals.' Jessie's face beamed.

'Are you okay with that arrangement, Cole?' Hope noticed he didn't say much at the table.

'Sure, sounds good to me. The sun is on our side too.' He sat looking like a cat that had found the cream.

***

They took off along the sandy banks of the glacial fed Dart River on horses that were trying to take the bit in their mouths. The fresh alpine air invigorated them as they trotted through the shallow waters. Then Hope encouraged Cole to do some river crossings and embrace the cool glacial waters.

'Don't go too far ahead, Hope. Stay near me. If you fall into the river I'll have to save you again.' He gave her a half smile.

Hope felt flattered with his gallantry but took umbrage at being held back when she was on Misty. She held her tongue for fear of scaring him off.

'Look at that spectacular view of Mount Aspiring.' As she looked up, a falcon swooped down into the tussock in front of her and startled Misty. The horse baulked sideways. Hope gripped her saddle hard and squeezed her thighs tight to stabilise herself.

'See what I mean!' Cole pushed his horse alongside her. 'Remember what that neurologist told you, that you won't survive another head injury.' He wiped beads of sweat from his forehead.

Hope couldn't hold back any longer.

176

'Cole! You really have to stop this. I'm a skilled rider and Misty is a good horse. She only fell up there on the ridge because it was steep and her foot went into a rabbit hole. Please— let's just continue this ride and let me enjoy it.'

As they walked the horses the rest of the way along the braided, dry stone river beds, a myriad of colour appeared. There was an abundance of pink and purple lupins which were a welcoming sight after passing the harsh mountainous landscape covered with nothing but tussock grass. They gave the horses a long rein as they made their way along the long windy riverbank.

'Hey—wait! Look over there.' Cole pointed to a pair of waterfowls that were frightened by the horses.

'They are Blue Ducks or Waterfowls and their bills have turned pink because we startled them. I learned all about them when I did my Agriscience Degree.'

Hope pulled Misty to a halt, captured by the surrounding eye-catching panorama. 'Isn't this river water an unusual emerald blue? I've never seen that in the North Island.'

'That's because of the glacial rock and silt that has come down from the mountains called glacial flour.'

'You're a fountain of knowledge, Cole Digby.'

With that, he instantly sat taller in the saddle and placed his hand on his thigh, as if imitating Wyatt Earp with his buckskin Stetson and high leather boots.

Hope looked past him, mesmerised by the view of Mount Aspiring against the clear blue sky.

'Come on, let's do the river crossing now as the horses are chaffing at the bit. You go first and I'll follow behind.' Hope pointed towards the river.

Cole gathered his reins and gave his horse a gentle nudge with his heel. With trepidation, he headed into the water with Hope in pursuit into the river shallows. Both horses frolicked by lifting a front leg in the air then splashing it down hard on the water. After a short time of walking the horses slowly across the river, they stopped on the other side to rest.

Hope looked back over her shoulder then turned Misty around. 'Let's go up into the Red Beech forest up there. There's a lovely bridle path that'll take us back near the ranch.'

They arrived back at the homestead before dusk, climbed off their horses, and rubbed their steaming backs down with wet towels. They continued their catch-up chat while removing the horses' bridles and letting them out into their grazing paddock.

'What a pity you won't be here when I start my new riding course. You could have given me a hand.'

'Yes, I know what you mean.' He flashed her a warm smile. 'It's a jolly nuisance my having to stay on at the orchard. It's been far too long now.'

'Dad will need you in the breeding program soon. Did I tell you Misty's foal was sired by that gorgeous white Arab stallion? You're missing out on seeing her grow.'

'Don't you worry— I'll be leaving the orchard as soon as Larry is back on his feet.'

They walked indoors just in time for a piping hot lamb stew that Myra had just placed on the table.

'Why don't you all sit in the lounge with a cold glass of ginger beer while the stew cools a bit.'

Hope pulled out a few bottles of the ginger beer she and her mother had recently bottled.

'How did you go today, Jessie? Did you enjoy feeding the foals?' Hope glanced at Jessie.

'It was awesome and they're so cute, especially that strawberry-roan. But that didn't take your Mum and me long. She told me I could go for a ride around the ranch, but in the end, Mack took me on a guided tour. He showed me all the horses and gave me a little history about each one, how your father the horse whisperer had broken each one of them in.'

'Really? And all that time I was beating myself up for leaving you back at the ranch.'

'You shouldn't have … actually— Mack is a really decent kind of guy, I quite like him.'

'Say no more, Jessie before I read between the lines.' Hope playfully tugged on Jessie's blond ponytail.

'I guess you might like to come and stay again during the next semester eh?'

'Well, I'm not going to say no, in fact, Mack asked if I was going to come for another holiday.'

'Good old Mack. You're right, he's a gem, and I can't understand why he's still single. He's quite shy, I guess. But he's not my type.'

'Ah— but I think we already know what your type is.' She gave Hope a mischievous smile and excused herself to go and get washed up as dinner was served.

Chapter Eighteen

Hope fell flat when Cole went back to Nelson. She felt mixed up, not sure whether she was in love with him or just missing his companionship. How would she know if she was in love? She'd never been in a serious relationship before.

'What do you want to do today, Jessie? Dad suggested we go for a ride out to Diamond Lake. It's beautiful and remote and we may see the wild horses.'

'That would be amazing. Isn't that where you had your accident? It might upset you going back there.'

'No way. I love going to the lake and it doesn't worry me at all to see the wild horses. It was just a freak accident and could have happened anywhere.'

Jessie was always so considerate and attentive which is what Hope liked so much about her friend.

'I'll ask Mum if she'll put together a packed lunch for us. Bring your camera just in case the horses are down by the lake.'

As Joel came inside the house, he overheard Hope telling her mother where they were going. 'Be careful at the lake. Promise you won't go up onto the ridge. We don't want any more rescue helicopters carting either of you off now do we?'

'Of course, we won't, Dad. I'm hoping Jessie will get to see a wild horse down by the lake.'

'Well— make sure you get back before dark.'

'Please don't fuss, Dad. I'm twenty-one and independent. Honest, we'll be okay.'

Joel knew he needed to back off, and like Myra, he too had trouble letting Hope grow up since her accident.

The school holidays were over and there were few people at the lake. The girls rode around to a spot where they had a good view of the bush and beech trees and the wild horses usually roamed. They dismounted and led the horses to the edge of the lake to drink then secured their reins to a large log which lay on the stony shore.

'Here, Jessie. Help me spread out this blanket on that grassy patch over there.' Hope dragged the blanket onto the grass.

'I'm famished. Let's tuck in.' Jessie unpacked the picnic box from her saddlebag.

They ate their food and lay on the grass waiting for the sun to appear. They were hoping to bask in its warmth but it was obscured by low clouds.

'Tell me about your boyfriend you've been seeing at university.' Hope rolled onto her front prodding Jessie in the ribs.

'Oh, him. I don't know if he's really my boyfriend. We've just been going out together for a few months. It's kind of platonic, I guess. He's doing the same Veterinary Science degree and in his final year like me.'

'Jessie— quick! Get your camera. Look up there.'

Hope pointed in the direction of a small clump of beech trees. That's where a well-trodden pathway led through the bush and the wild horses were often seen. Just then, in full view, a majestic golden palomino stallion made its way down to the water's edge followed by a palomino mare with its foal. The mare was a little nervous, unlike the bold stallion which was undeterred by a few cars and tourists near the lakeside. Jessie took one photo after another.

'What a pity you and your Dad aren't able to bring down the herd. Do you think he'll have another go at it?'

'No, he can't do that, it's illegal now. Soon after my accident, a Bill was passed for the protection of feral horses and it's against the law to take them out of their natural environment.'

'I didn't know that. When I look at them over there, I can see how vulnerable they are. What about poachers and hunters?'

'Hunters aren't allowed in this area where the horses are breeding. They have designated areas now, as there are other animals that are protected too.'

They sat still, soaking up the awesome spectacle of these beautiful beasts as Jessie thanked God for the privilege of watching this little family. A stallion, mare and foal— a witness to her creator's wonderful handiwork.

The sun began to sink gracefully behind the Humboldt Mountains as the horses quietly disappeared into the beech forest.

'Come on, Jessie, we'd better get going back home as it'll be dark soon. You'll have to come here again during your next semester break.'

'I'll look forward to that. I'm going to miss this amazing place. No wonder they call it Paradise. It'll be sad to have to say goodbye to it all tomorrow. Who knows, maybe one day I can move down here. When did you say your vet was going to retire?'

'Are you serious?'

'I'm working part-time in a local vet's clinic. Who knows what the future holds. I know I'm part of a divine plan, though I'm just not sure what that is right now.'

***

'Are you awake, Hope?' There was a gentle tap on her door as she lay in bed rubbing her eyes, disturbed by the bright sunlight streaming through the crack in her blinds.

'Mum— what's wrong?'

'Nothing's wrong, dear. It's your old employer Jock wanting to talk to you. Maybe he wants you to go back and work for him. Quick, he's waiting on the phone in the lounge.'

Hope scrambled out to the lounge in her pyjamas, half asleep. When she finished her conversation with Jock and hung up the phone, she looked for her mother who was out the front feeding the hens.

'Mum— He asked if we are doing anything tomorrow and would we like to go to Corriedale Hills Station for lunch. He wants to meet you and Dad, as his son Hamish is needing some training in breaking horses. He wants to discuss it with Dad as he heard that he's the expert around here.'

'Really? That sounds interesting. Go and ask your father if he's able to go up there tomorrow. He's in the barn sorting out feed for the horses.'

As she wandered over towards the barn, she remembered her long conversations with Charity, Jock's daughter and the kindness she and the family had shown her when she'd worked for them. The only family member who was an unknown quantity was Hamish their son whom she'd not yet met.

'Can we go up there tomorrow, Dad ... please? I'd love to see them again as I've only spoken to Charity once over the phone

183

since I left. I think it would be great for you and me to help Hamish learn to break horses.'

'Oh, you do, do you? Who said you'll be involved?' He rubbed the stubble on his chin, hiding the smile on his lips with his hand.

'What ... why? You know I can break in a horse almost as well as you can now!'

'Hah! I thought I might get a reaction. I think you and I could well be a good team.' He couldn't hide the twinkle in his eyes nor could she hide the way her face lit up with elation when her father made her feel special.

***

'It's not far from here, Dad. Just over that ridge and we'll be there.'

Hope pointed in the direction of Corriedale Hills Station. She opened the car's window and appeared almost mesmerised as she gazed at the breath-taking views across the valley of rich fertile pastures covered with sheep that extended for miles. She took in a deep breath. 'Isn't it awesome? I just love looking at the view from here. See the lake down there.'

'The view's certainly beautiful.' Myra craned her neck then also rolled down her window.

'There it is! That's the station down there. Just go down that long driveway with the poplar trees.'

They arrived on time and Gilly opened the door with Jock in tow. They welcomed Hope with open arms, a degree of warmth far removed from one's usual employers.

'Lovely to meet you both finally'. They shook hands with Joel and Myra.

'Hope was such a blessing to us when she worked here— she must certainly be a light in your lives.' Gilly showed them to a

184

seat in the lounge. She offered her guests fresh scones with home-made raspberry jam and asparagus rolls. A teapot with willow pattern stood on a trolley next to them with a jug of orange juice. 'Let me pour you tea.'

'Just milk for both of us thanks. What about you, Hope?' Joel nodded at Hope.

'Orange juice thanks. I'm feeling dehydrated.'

'Jock, where's Hamish? He said he'd be here to meet our guests.' Gilly looked out the window then shook her head. 'He's not the best timekeeper but I'm sure he'll be along soon.'

They all became engrossed in deep conversations, learning all about Hope's accident and their experiences with the Kaimanawa horses. Jock and Myra even disclosed the fact that they had been childhood sweethearts and had recently married. That didn't go down that well. Hope noticed that Jock and Gilly appeared awkward, glancing at each other sideways. But Hope knew them well and did not believe they would judge them.

There was a rattle at the back door, and the thud of leather boots being dropped on the floor. An unfamiliar face appeared in the doorway of the lounge.

'Sorry, Mum. I didn't realise what time it was.'

Hamish introduced himself to Joel and Myra and lifted his Stetson to Hope then placed it on a side table. Hope sat there open-mouthed, gaping at the tall, broad-shouldered young man with thick black hair that contrasted his dark blue eyes. She looked away, as he glanced back at her, obviously aware of her reaction.

He yanked up his new-looking blue denim jeans, tucking his black tee-shirt inside the waist and sat on the end of the couch next to his father.

Joel spoke first. 'Your father tells me you're ready to start breaking horses. Hope here is pretty good at this too. I'd like to involve her in your training if you're happy to start soon.'

Joel hadn't noticed the body language between Hamish and Hope. She felt her throat go dry and her voice sounded raspy as Hamish turned to address her.

'Oh, so you're also a horse whisperer?' Hamish threw her a glance that made her feel as though his intense blue eyes were piercing her soul.

She took a sip of juice. 'Ah, no. Dad's the horse whisperer and I'm just his accomplice.'

'Aw, Hope. Don't be so modest. I'd say that you probably don't need me around when you're breaking any horse in. You're a horse magnet. They go to you like bees to honey,' said Joel, flashing his daughter the warmest smile.

Hamish continued to fix his eyes on Hope while Joel paid tribute to his daughter.

'Come on— perhaps we can show you the horse if you'd like to check her out first.' Jock stood up and showed them out the back.

'Would you like me to show you my garden, Myra? I heard you're an avid gardener at the ranch.' Gilly smiled warmly at Myra and led her onto the deck and down a path that displayed a huge vegetable patch and an English country garden in full colour.

Hope followed the men out to the paddocks where the horses grazed. As they wandered towards the gate, Joel and Jock chatted away while Hamish kept looking back over his shoulder, while Hope lagged behind. He waited for her to catch up.

In a stockyard nearby, stood a remarkable looking Cremello mare pawing at the dusty ground as if bored or frustrated. As

Hope approached the gate to look closer at her, the mare stopped pounding the ground and glanced up at Hope. She was captivated by the animal's mysterious pale blue eyes and imagined how amazing this mare would be for breeding.

Her father interrupted her thoughts. 'What do you think? Gorgeous, isn't she? Three years old and never been ridden. Hamish is hoping, with your help, that he'll be able to saddle her.'

'Is that right, Hamish? I think that's possible and Hope's keen to help you with the basics.' Joel gave Hope a nod.

She felt her throat tighten with a strange kind of discomfort at Joel drawing Hamish's attention to her.

'I'll bet she takes to you like a duck to water.' Hamish flashed her a warm smile.

'No, it's you she needs to take to and bond with. I can just show you how to do it. What's her name?'

'I call her Champagne ... when can you start training her, Hope?'

She looked at her father, waiting for him to reply.

'Oh, Hope won't be able to help you train her until I have handled her first. You'll need me for the initial training of your horse to see how she's going to handle. Hope and I'll work together to start with. She can take over once I see how the horse behaves.'

Joel walked into the pen to see the horse's reaction. He walked around her a few times then left the pen again.

'She's quite calm for an unbroken youngster. Do you spend much time with her?' He looked over at Hamish.

'Yes, I do regularly. I bring her in here with a halter to give her hard feed. I just wasn't sure how to get her to take the bit. I tried to get the bridle on her but she spooked every time.'

'That's not the way to do it. I can see you need some instruction, my boy.' Joel winked at Jock and Hope could see that Hamish didn't take kindly to being called a boy in front of her.

'You've done really well Hamish by getting a halter on her and she's already bonded with you, I can see,' said Hope, coming to his rescue.

Hamish walked inside the pen to give Champagne some pellets from his pocket.

'Good girl.' He rubbed her neck as the horse licked his other hand.

'Well, folks, let's get back to the house and talk brass tacks. We'll have to discuss your schedule and put a plan together, I guess'. Jock removed his hat, scratched his head, and walked back to the house with Joel.

Hamish chose to stay back behind them and take the opportunity to talk with Hope.

'Would you like to come with me to take her back to her grazing paddock?' He stood still, studying Hope's face.

'Sure— I'd love to.'

'Dad! We'll be at the house shortly.' Hamish called out to his father.

When they were finally all together back in the lounge, Joel sat next to Hamish with a diary on his lap.

'How about if I come here each morning with Hope for a week. We'll leave early and be back at our ranch by midday to do some work. After that, Hope can come alone for the following week. Hope's still busy with her own mare, Misty's new foal. She starts her new riding course in two weeks. Another little side business she has.'

'How will you manage your ranch if you are both up here so much?' Jock looked across at Joel.

'I have a quiet time at the ranch this month. There are no mares about to birth until later in the year. I'm expecting my best ranch hand, Cole to return soon. He's an asset to the ranch and can help me catch up with the work. I've got behind a bit since he's been away, but it's okay while it's quiet.' Joel had his head in his diary as he spoke. 'When my casual ranch hands return they'll do some hay baling for me.'

Hope's cheeks burned at the mention of Cole returning. She looked at Gilly. 'Would I be able to have a glass of water, please? I must be dehydrated.'

'Of course Hope. It's warm out there today.' Gilly brought out a jug of water from the kitchen. Hope's face was still flushed.

'Well, that's settled then. We'll expect you both Monday at nine if all goes well.' Jock shook Joel's hand and patted Hope on the shoulder. 'I'll be paying your travel expenses, of course.'

Hamish gave Joel his hand then stood awkwardly facing Hope. 'Look forward to seeing … um … to having you come on board with us, Hope,' he uttered.

Gilly hugged Myra and Hope. 'It's a pity you didn't meet Charity this time both of you. Next time she's home I must get you all back for another visit.'

On her way out, Myra stood in the hallway glancing at a photo of Charity hanging on the wall. 'I think it's our turn. You must all come to us next time.'

As Joel drove the car down the tree-studded driveway onto the rough country road, Hope went quiet, in deep thought. It was as though she was struggling with some kind of inner conflict.

'Well, Hope, what do you think? Are you still keen on these arrangements with Hamish?' Joel furtively winked at his wife.

'It'll require quite a bit of travel. I'll pay your wages, of course. This is all part of our business and as my business partner, you get half of our horse-breaking contracts. Jock has offered me a handsome price to break in Champagne for Hamish who wants to use her for showing.'

'Now that you put it that way, I'm super keen!' She couldn't hide the fact that the monetary offer was not the key magnet for her being eager to spend the next few weeks visiting Corriedale Hills Station.

***

As Hope started on her meal, her mother looked at her husband and gave him a nod.

'Hope— we had a phone call this evening you may like to know about.' Her father tried to cover his wry smile with his hand.

'Ah— was it Jessie? I was wondering when I would hear from her. Is she going to phone back?'

'No, well ... actually, it wasn't Jessie at all.'

'Who then ... Doug, I suppose? I haven't written to him in a while.'

Myra kept her gaze on Hope's face as her father spoke.

'Oh, Joel. Don't keep her hanging like that. Go on and tell her.' Myra frowned at him.

'It was Cole. I'd spoken to him on the phone last week to see if he was any closer to coming back to work and he said he would phone back once he knows.'

'Really.' Hope went into her coy mode.

'Well— is he?' Her eyes suddenly sprang open like whirlpools and her heart missed a beat.

190

'Yes, my dear. He's arriving at the end of the month and just in time. I was about to employ another qualified horseman to help me. To tell you the truth, it's been a long haul running the breeding program alone.'

'At last— the ranch will get back to normal. And when he's not with you, Dad, he might help me with my program too. Some of the riders in the next lot of classes want to learn how to break in a horse. I should be finished up on Corriedale Hills Station by then.'

'That's good to hear. Cole's had a good teacher— in me of course and has become an expert in horse breaking techniques. They couldn't get a better trainer apart from me ... and you.' Joel squeezed her neck affectionately.

'It's good news, Dad. I'm looking forward to seeing him back here again.'

Hope filled the bath to the brim with hot water and bubble bath. The foam almost overflowed onto the floor. She undressed then opened the bathroom window wide so that she could see the cobalt-blue carpet of bright stars. The full silver moon illuminated the sky above the house.

She climbed into the cast iron claw bath carefully lowering herself down and sighed at the soothing effect of the silky smooth warm water that saturated her body. She stretched out long like a cat and lay her head back on the sill of the bath. As she stared at the dazzling constellation above, her eyes stayed transfixed on the moon as if her God was there, watching over her.

'What does my future hold, Lord? I'd love to have a glimpse of it,' she uttered. Then a song kept resounding in her mind and she started to sing, 'Que será, será. Whatever will be, will be. My future's not ours to see, que será, será.'

Chapter Nineteen

Hope helped her mother prepare breakfast with an eagerness in her spirit. Today is a special day. For the first time, she'll be coaching her new client, Hamish Weston to break in his horse. Joel will be at her side but she'll be doing the teaching herself.

'You'd better get a move on, Hope. Finish your toast and I'll meet you out at the Ute. We said we would be there by nine.'

'Okay, Dad. I'll be out in a few minutes.'

She rushed her coffee and the remains of her toast with Myra's popular strawberry jam. She kissed her mother and rushed out the door licking her fingers.

Joel drove cautiously around the deceptive bends in the icy road that was lethal during the spring thaw.

'Have I told you lately how proud I am that you're now taking on private clients? You've become quite a businesswoman. You'll be able to take over this ranch one day when I'm an old man.'

'Aw, thanks, Dad. I hope this contract at Corriedale Hills Station will only take two weeks as you said. My new group of riding students starts after that. I'll have to be back by then.'

'You'll just have to make sure you do a great job of training Hamish so that you won't have to go back up there.' He winked at her playfully.

Hope wasn't sure how to answer that and kept quiet.

The Westons were pleased to see them, especially Hamish who scurried out to greet them in the driveway.

'We're all ready. Champagne's in the stockyard waiting for you.' He stood beaming at Hope while her father chuckled quietly.

***

By the end of the week, Joel had taken Hamish through the basic handling techniques for an unbroken horse. Mainly he just initiated the main rudiments then Hope reinforced them.

The first week of your lessons has gone quickly, Hamish. You've worked hard at it!' Joel shook Hamish's hand.

'Thanks to you both. I appreciate you coming and giving up precious time from the ranch.'

Joel turned back to Hope. 'I must say we're a good team, Hope, and I.'

'Thanks' Dad. I guess we'll see the results by the end of the two weeks.'

'Champagne has a quiet temperament for an unbroken mare. She's taken to the bit and bridle easily.' Joel patted the horse's nose gently.

Hamish turned to Joel. 'I reckon you showing me how to bond with her in the pen first off, made all the difference, Joel. I think that's why they call you a horse whisperer.'

Joel laughed. 'You two talk about your arrangements for next week. I'm going into the house to discuss some business with Jock before we leave. Alright, Hope?'

'Sure, Dad. See you out by the car shortly.'

Hope's face gleamed when her father disappeared around the corner.

'I remember your father saying that his services wouldn't be required during the second week when we start saddling Champagne. Are you coming on your own then?'

'I guess so unless he changes his mind. That's if he thinks Champagne is ready to be saddled.'

'I'll look forward to that … I mean to Champagne being saddled. Everything's gone better than I expected. And you are pretty good at handling a horse, I might add.' Hamish nodded at her, his unusually white teeth glinting under a broad smile.

'You've also worked Champagne well. I reckon you're a fast learner.'

'Thanks. I'll see you back here on Monday.'

Hamish walked tall, broad shoulders pulled back and head high as they walked back to the house. Hope liked the idea of a confident strong male walking alongside her. Particularly one as handsome as Hamish.

'Wait, Hope. I've something for you. I'll just run to the barn and get it.'

He rushed off while Hope saw Joel walking out to the Ute. She walked back towards the house as Hamish approached her with something in his hands.

'I want you to have this.' He handed her an exquisite hand-quilted saddle blanket with vibrant colours. 'My grandmother made it for me when I was given my first horse. I want you to have it.'

Hopes face turned the colour of the red geranium by the front door. She was lost for words. 'I don't know what to say … it's gorgeous. But don't you think you should hold onto this? It's very special.'

'I've had it for ages and it's time for a change. It's a gift for being so patient with me. I know you've gone the extra mile to teach me.'

'It's a wonderful gift. I need a new one. Thank you!' She wanted to kiss him on the cheek but didn't want to give him the wrong idea. Soon Cole will return to Dart River Ranch. She's kept her heart for him all this time, even though he doesn't know it.

'I've got to go, Dad's waiting. See you next week then.' She waved at Hamish as he saw them off in their Ute.

As Joel drove out onto the main road, he couldn't hold back. 'He seems to be quite a decent sort of guy. I think he's a bit smitten with you, Hope. Or am I wrong?'

Hope chose to remain silent, trying to deal with the discomfort of her father raising a sensitive subject.

'What do you think, Dad? Have I done all right this week? Are you happy about me taking Hamish through the saddling and mounting techniques next time?'

'Happy? I'm over the moon with your progress. I probably didn't need to be there the whole week. You don't need me around anymore with your skills.'

'Great! I think I can manage on my own now. Look at this saddle blanket that Hamish gave me.'

Joel's eyes darted to the blanket and back on the road. 'I think it took a lot for him to give that away. I would guard my heart if I were you. Oh, by the way, Cole is due back anytime.' As he said this, he kept looking at her body language, but again she said nothing. She's heard that so many times before that he's coming back. What if he doesn't? She clammed up for the rest of the trip home.

***

As Hope drove up to Corriedale Hills Station the following Monday, her stomach churned with both excited expectation and anxiety.

How does she know that Hamish is to be trusted? She hardly knows him. Her thoughts cautioned her. *Please, God, give me the discernment I need. I'm attracted to Hamish and he appears besotted with me, but I'm fond of my dear friend Cole as well. I need some kind of sign whether to get involved on a romantic level with Hamish.*

As she drove towards the house, Hamish was waiting to greet her with a disarming smile. She couldn't help but flash him a broad smile in return. She was impressed with his appearance. He was dressed in what appeared to be new tan suede pants and a blue and white check shirt. He tipped his Stetson towards her and walked with her to Champagne's pen.

'This is your big day, Hamish. I think Champagne is ready to be saddled but we need to do it in stages.' Hamish picked up his saddle and placed it across his shoulders.

'Today we just use a saddle blanket for mounting so you won't be needing her saddle.'

'Oh, I see. I'll just put this back over the wooden perch then.'

Hope walked on while he placed the saddle back in the shed. She wandered up to the pen where Champagne stood impatiently to be let out and called her. At first, the mare just stood at a distance glaring at her, ears pricked and alert. She started pawing the dusty ground.

Hope took a carrot from her jacket pocket. 'Here you are. Come and see me.' Champagne gave a soft whinny and trotted towards her, stopping directly in front of her. She stretched her neck over the top rail of the fence and took the carrot from Hope.

Hope felt a hand on her shoulder and cringed slightly. Hamish took a step back. 'I can see she's taken a liking to you. I hope she'll be just as amicable when I jump on her back.'

'There won't be any jumping on her back, at least not for the time being. It's going to be a gradual, gentle process. You go in the pen with her and I'll stand still while I give you instructions.'

'Ooh—that's what I like, a woman in control.'

Hope tried to hide her awkwardness.

'Sorry—just teasing. I didn't mean to embarrass you,' he chuckled.

'Let's get started.' Hope said, not knowing how to reply.

Hamish started exercising the horse with the long reins. After a short time, the mare had made good contact, bonding with him.

'Now place your saddle blanket on her back quietly as you go and once she is accepting it, lean in on her shoulder for a few minutes until she trusts you.'

Within no time, Hamish was able to slide over her back, straddling himself crossways, draping his head over one side and his legs down the other. Within the next hour, he was able to sit on her back without her bucking.

'Shall we stop for lunch now? Don't you want a break,' he asked Hope.

'No! Sorry, we can't stop right now. You have to keep going while she has accepted you on her back. We can introduce the saddle now. I'll get it for you from the perch. Just stay with her and keep the contact but stay off her.'

By the end of the afternoon, Champagne had accepted the saddle and stopped bucking.

'That's it for today. Tomorrow you can try to saddle her straight away and maybe by the end of the day you may be riding her, saddle and all.'

Hope was exhausted. She'd half expected Champagne to buck Hamish off which would not happen if Joel was doing the teaching. But she'd been surprised that the techniques that Joel had drummed into her were getting results and she was now becoming a successful horse whisperer too.

'Hope, I've been meaning to ask you something.' Hamish leaned on the bonnet of her car with his elbow, looking her in the eye.

'The annual hootenanny hoe-down barn dance shindig at the Kingston Hall is on this Saturday night. I haven't anyone to bring and was hoping that you might accompany me as a kind of celebration of Champagne passing her test-ride.' His eyes didn't leave her face.

'Oh, I see. Umm ... I don't know what to say.'

'Just say yes ... please, Hope. I'd love you to come. I'll talk to my folks. I'm sure you can sleep in Charity's room for the night as she's still away. Then you won't have to drive all the way home in the dark by yourself.'

Hope buckled under Hamish's unwavering persuasion. 'I suppose so. I'll check that my father hasn't any jobs lined up for me. We are partners in the ranch and I'm also running riding classes next week. I'll let you know before Friday.'

As Hope drove home after a long day, she felt pangs of guilt, disloyalty at the thought that she might be betraying Cole, even though they weren't in any kind of official relationship. He's not even made his intentions known to her yet. She'd not been to a dance since her twenty-first birthday and was eager to let her hair down.

That evening in front of the fire, Hope sat stroking the old cat, trying to decide whether to disclose to her parents that change that was in the wind.

'You seem to be miles away, Hope. Come on, what's up?' Joel looked from Hope to Myra and back again, observing the intense expression on their daughter's face, her eyes like blue marbles, staring into the fire.

'Oh, sorry! Just a bit weary from today's efforts.'

'Well, you can give yourself a hug. You've almost caught up to me with your horse whispering. Soon I won't be needed around here.' His eyes smiled.

'But there's something else— want to tell us anything?'

'Oh, Dad. You're so persistent.'

'Leave her alone, Joel. She's worn out.' Myra pulled on his arm.

'What is it, Hope? Did something else happen up at the station?' Joel persevered.

'Not exactly happen—it's Hamish. He desperately wants me to go to a dance this Saturday.'

'Dance ... which one is this?' Myra sat on the edge of her seat suddenly coming to life.

'I think it's called the annual hootenanny hoe-down barn dance shindig held in Kingston Hall.'

'That's a mouthful,' Joel burst into a loud guffaw.

'I know. Hilarious isn't it?' Hope giggled.

'He said he doesn't have anyone else to ask, which I find hard to believe from a guy as good looking as he is.'

'I suppose it can't do you any harm. You don't need our permission. You're an adult now and most young women your age have left home. You would have done so too if you'd not been tied up with the business or had an accident.'

Joel tossed the cat off his lap and put another log on the fire. He slipped into his slippers and flopped back into his well-worn armchair.

'He seems to be a decent guy. Why not go and have some fun for a change. Life has been a bit too serious lately.' Myra handed them both a mug of hot cocoa.

'I wish I was your age again going to a hootenanny hoe-down barn dance shindig.' Joel held his stomach, letting out a roar of laughter again and Myra couldn't contain herself either.

***

By the end of the week, the day before the barn dance, Hamish was already up in the saddle, trotting Champagne around the riding ménage. Hope had spent all day going over some basic dressage techniques.

'I think I'm just about done here. You have all the skills you need now, Hamish. You just have to practice them.'

'Sure, thanks to your expert teaching. I must say I couldn't have had a better teacher to take me through the drill.'

'Yes, you could ... my father. He's the best horse whisperer for miles around here.'

'Oh, that's true, but you come a close second, I'm sure. Hold on—I nearly forgot. Mum said to ask you to stay for dinner. Are you all set to come and stay over tomorrow night after the dance?'

'Yes, I think so. I don't know if I have anything to wear yet. I haven't had time to look.'

'I'm pretty certain that you'll look beautiful, no matter what you wear.'

Hope noticed a glint of delight in his eyes as he spoke.

'Come on, let's go eat. Mum has dinner ready.'

As they walked to the house, Hamish draped his arms around Hope's neck. He's taking liberties. Why is he acting so familiar when he's really just a business client?

The mealtime with the Westons was awkward for Hope this time. She was sure Hamish's parents thought there was a budding romance in the air. No one had thought of asking her whether she had a boyfriend or a person of interest in her life, not once. Not even Hamish.

'Have some more of that lemon pie, Hope. Your mother said you are partial to it. You can take some home with you if you like.' Gilly handed her the dish and Hamish stayed fixated on her.

'Oh, no thanks. It's really delicious but I won't fit into my dress tomorrow night.' Instantly she wished she hadn't drawn attention to the dance.

'Dear me. We can't let that happen and have you not turning up. Hamish hasn't stopped talking about taking you to the dance, all week.'

Hamish's face turned florid as he flashed his mother a disapproving glare. Hope pitied him being embarrassed in front of his new date.

Hamish stood up. 'Let's go for a walk outside, I love this spring weather.' Hope followed him out the back.

'Your Mum sure has a beautiful garden.' Hope bent over to sniff one of a multitude of deep red roses.

Hamish stooped forward. He picked one of the large blooms.
'Here, this matches your complexion. Just to say thank you for all
your patience and tolerance while teaching me.'

'Remember I said you've already given me that gorgeous
saddle blanket. And your father has paid Dad for the job. I'll be
keeping my cut from that too.'

'Well, just to say thank you again to a special lady.' He threw
her another one of his charming smiles.

'Look—Hamish … oh, don't worry.' Hope wanted to tell
Hamish she was already spoken for and lost her nerve.

What if I put Hamish off then find out Cole has cooled off me?

'Thank you. I've got to get going back now. I have an early start
tomorrow. I'll just say goodbye to your parents.'

'Sorry I can't drop around and pick you up tomorrow night.
You're staying with us the night so at least you don't have to drive
back home afterwards. I'll meet you at the hall around seven.
Look forward to dancing with you.' The Cheshire cat grin did not
leave his face.

Hope put her foot down hard and zoomed down the driveway
and out the gate. Lucky for her, Hamish said he'd shut the gate,
so she drove down the road like a mad thing. Why was she
beginning to feel cornered? He's only wanting to dance with her
because there's no one else.

Thirty minutes into the journey home, the rose lay on the edge
of the seat beginning to droop in the heat of the car. 'Is this a
sign, God? Please let me know', she uttered.

Chapter Twenty

As her car veered around the corner and down the long driveway to her home, she braked suddenly. Hesitating before parking her car in its usual spot, she saw a familiar sight that she'd not seen in a while. It was Coles red pickup parked next to the cottage which had recently become vacant.

He's home! Why didn't anyone warn her? She wouldn't have agreed to accompany Hamish to the stupid dance.

'Hope—just in time for dinner. Why don't you go and freshen up? We have a visitor arriving for the evening. I think you may want to change.' Her mother stood in the doorway pointing in the direction of Cole's cottage.

'I've already eaten at the Weston's. I know he's back, Mum. Why didn't you tell me he was coming? This is embarrassing.' Her face spelt annoyance.

'We didn't know either. He wasn't due until the end of this month but he drove down from Nelson today to surprise us ... or you, I guess.'

'But I have this barn dance to go to tomorrow.'

'That's okay. Just tell him you are staying with the Westons and will be back on Sunday. You don't have to elaborate.'

'Thanks Mum. I wouldn't have known what to say—I mean ...
I'm not lying.'

Joel and Myra held the floor during the meal, to Hope's relief.
Myra had already explained to Cole that Hope had eaten because
his visit was to have been a surprise for her. Cole told them all
about the orchard and how hard he'd worked for his father and
brother.

'I don't like orchard work. It's not for me. I missed the ranch so
much you've no idea. Especially ... the horses,' he spewed out.

Joel flashed Myra a grin and did not dare glance back at Hope.
Myra stifled a titter.

'Let's go for a stroll, Hope. I need to walk off your mother's
unbeatable cooking. I'd like to see how Misty's foal has grown.

'I suppose I could let you both off the dishes, just this once.'
Myra teased.

'Thanks Mrs G.' Cole strutted out to where Misty and foal
grazed, his head held high as he strode across the field in his
smart western attire. His skin appeared even more bronzed than
his previous return home. Hope couldn't help making furtive spot
checks of him.

They went back inside for coffee then Hope said goodbye to
him on the doorstep.

'Any plans this Saturday? I thought perhaps that we could go
into Queenstown for the evening. I'd like to take you to dinner.
We've a lot of catching up to do.'

This is just what she's been dreading—being put on the spot!

'I ... ah... I'm going to be staying with the Westons tomorrow
evening sorry, I've already committed myself.'

'Are you? That's the people you've been helping to break in
their mare.'

'How did you know?'

'Your father told me over the phone a few weeks ago. Are you still working with the horse then?'

'No, that contract has just ended today. I think they just wanted to pamper me to say thank you. The Westons really like me and they were so good to me when I worked for them and lived in.'

She hoped he wouldn't ask any more questions. She just wouldn't have been able to lie.

'Perhaps we can go for a ride when I get back on Sunday. I'm going to miss church anyway this weekend.'

'Sure, I'll catch you up on Sunday then.' He gave her a warm smile and went back to his cottage.

Hope went inside and slumped in an armchair. Joel was busy stacking wood beside the fireplace.

'What happened out there? I thought you two were having a good time catching up. Why the sad face?'

'I'm in a pickle, Dad. Now that Cole's back, I don't want to go to the dance with Hamish. I'd like to pull out of it but Hamish is looking forward to taking me, I know he is. I don't want to hurt him.'

'Perhaps you should be really honest with Hamish and tell him you have a boyfriend who has just arrived home.'

'What, Dad? What do you mean my boyfriend? Cole's just a friend, although a dear friend.'

'My dear Hope. I think you need to get real and realise that Cole is besotted with you. Can't you see that? Each time he phoned from Nelson, he interrogated me about you.'

'Why didn't you tell me? I didn't know.'

'I thought there was no point with him being so far away and not knowing when he'd return.'

'If only it was Cole who'd asked me to the dance. I don't want to go now.'

Joel walked over and took her hand. 'Listen to me. Honesty is the best policy. I think you should phone Hamish and explain the whole situation to him and apologise. Say you didn't know Cole would be giving you a surprise visit and that you thought he'd given you up after being up north for so long. Say that you'd misjudged the situation with Cole and you need to put it right with both of them.'

Hope took her father's advice on board and picked up the phone to ring Hamish.

'Hi, Hamish. There's something I need to talk to you about.' With a knot in her stomach that felt like a heavy stone, she told it exactly as Joel had suggested.

'I can't say I'm not disappointed, Hope. But I'm really pleased you've been honest with me. I know I've been a bit to blame, being so pushy. To be truthful, I've had a few offers to accompany local girls to the dance. Why don't you invite your friend, Cole? You can sit at my table with my dance partner and me if you like. Joel has talked about Cole quite a lot, I think I'd like to meet this fine horseman.'

'Thanks, Hamish for being so understanding. I really am sorry for mucking you around. Perhaps we'll still see you there then.'

Hope breathed a huge sigh of relief and slumped back into her chair by the fireplace.

'All worked out then, has it? I told you so. I think Cole's had his heart set on you for a very long time. And I think you feel the same way but haven't admitted it to yourself.'

'I know, Dad. You're right. I'll tell him this weekend. I can't wait to invite him to the dance tomorrow.' She felt a huge weight fall off her, telling herself the truth in her own mind. Now she just has to find the courage to tell Cole how she really feels.

***

The hootenanny hoe-down barn dance lived up to its name as a shindig—loud, boisterous and packed full of people kicking up their heels to the music of "I hear that train a coming" and such like. Hamish sat with an attractive redhead in the corner of the hall with Hope and Cole. There was a light-hearted atmosphere around the table and Hamish acted as if he wasn't bothered at all by his earlier disappointment. Hope observed his behaviour with interest as he became louder and more egotistical with every drop of drink. He sat there boasting about how he could break in a wild horse and that he was a horse whisperer and never mentioned Hope's name.

'I'm sick of watching him. Let's go outside for some fresh air.' Hope took Cole by the hand and led him outside. They found a seat on a bench in front of the hall.

'I'm so glad you could come here with me. I don't know what would have happened if I'd been here with Hamish on my own. His true colours have come out tonight.'

She caught a strong whiff of cigarette smoke that had drifted her way. She looked up and saw Hamish leaning on the girl's shoulders, blowing smoke over her head. He was inebriated, making a fool of himself swearing and acting common. This was so different to what Hope knew of him.

'Wow—how wrong I've been. One certainly can't judge a book by its cover.' She leaned her head against Cole's shoulder as he placed his arm around her and pulled her close. 'What do you mean?' He frowned and gave her a mystified glance.

'Oh, no matter. I'm just surprised to see Hamish drinking and smoking ... I had no idea.'

'Don't you worry about him. Let's just enjoy this lovely evening we have together.' He leaned his lips into hers and she responded warmly and yielded.

'Tell you what. Let's take off and drive around the lake to Queenstown for a bite to eat away from all this noise, just the two of us.'

It was a clear night, and in the abyss, over the lake, the stars seemed to sparkle brighter than ever. As they headed into Queenstown, a full moon appeared, silver and translucent revealing the ripples that the gentle breeze made on the water.

'Look, there's a Bistro still open and I can hear music, our kind of music.'

As they entered the Bistro, a strong whiff of a delicious aroma emanated from the kitchen.

'Is the food still on?' Cole asked the waiter.

'The kitchen is almost closing so put your order in now.'

They sat at a table eating a light meal while music from George Gershwin aided their digestion.

'A far cry from the boisterous hoe-down, don't you think?' Hope seemed to be on cloud nine as her eyes took on a dreamy appearance.

The music changed to lyrics from Frank Sinatra.

Cole jumped up and paid for the meal at the counter suddenly.

'What's happening, why the rush?' Hope's eyes widened.

'Come with me. Come on.'

He took her by the hand and led her across the street to where the car was parked. Instead of opening the passenger door to let her in, he kept on leading her down to the water's edge of the lake where there was flat freshly mown grass.

As the breeze caught the melody of "I Only Have Eyes for You", Cole started to slow dance with her, leaning his head into her neck.

Hope peaked out from under his head. She could see the bright moon rays dancing on the water and suddenly everything in the world appeared wonderfully surreal. He kissed her more passionately this time, his full lips sinking deep into her soft mouth, and her heart melted. They danced like this for a short time, although it seemed like hours until the music stopped.

Without any warning, Cole went down on his knees. Hope couldn't see what he was doing in the dark. Then she caught the glint of something shining in his hand in the moonlight. He slipped the diamond ring on her finger gently.

'Please, Hope, please marry me. I've been waiting for this day ever since I went to Nelson and this is the perfect moment to ask you. I've loved you for a very long time and it's great that we're such close friends. But I need more from our relationship.'

'I can't believe it. You just took the words out of my mouth. I never stopped thinking about you the whole time you were away and I almost gave up hope that you would return.'

They held each other tight and kissed as though they could never get enough of each other. The music started up again. This time it was Elvis Presley's "And I Love You So".

Hope was mesmerised, intoxicated by the music and Cole's voice. She whispered into his ear, 'Yes, of course I will. Why has it taken you so long?'

He pulled her closer. With this next deeply passionate kiss they became lost in a time warp. They continued to slow dance in the moonlight until the last song played.

After the music ended, the barman stood outside the door of the building and waved. Cole leaned over and spoke softly in Hope's ear. 'I had to bribe him to play our special music and turn up the volume so we could hear it over here.'

They walked to the car hand in hand while the wind in the willows whispered the promise of change, of good times to come.

****THE END****

www.ingramcontent.com/pod-product-compliance
Lightning Source LLC
Chambersburg PA
CBHW022144050726
47590CB00002B/570